B
TOPIA

BIKE
TOPIA
FEMINIST BICYCLE SCIENCE FICTION
STORIES IN EXTREME FUTURES

EDITED BY

ELLY BLUE

MICROCOSM PUBLISHING

PORTLAND, OR

BIKETOPIA
FEMINIST BICYCLE SCIENCE FICTION STORIES IN EXTREME FUTURES

Edited by Elly Blue

All content © its creators, 2016-2017

Final editorial content © Elly Blue, 2017

This edition © Elly Blue Publishing, an imprint of Microcosm Publishing, 2017

First printing, September 8, 2017

All work remains the property of the original creators.

ISBN 978-1-62106-206-6

Elly Blue Publishing, an imprint of Microcosm Publishing
2752 N Williams Ave.
Portland, OR 97227
TakingTheLane.com
MicrocosmPublishing.com

Cover art by Cecila Granata

This is the fourth volume in the *Bikes in Space* series. To find other volumes, or to submit your own feminist bicycle science fiction stories, go to bikesinspace.com

Find more feminist bicycle science fiction and many other titles at ellybluepublishing.com

If you bought this on Amazon, that sucks because you could have gotten it cheaper and supported a small, independent publisher at MicrocosmPublishing.com

Microcosm Publishing is Portland's most diversified publishing house and distributor with a focus on the colorful, authentic, and empowering. Our books and zines have put your power in your hands since 1996, equipping readers to make positive changes in their lives and in the world around them. Microcosm emphasizes skill-building, showing hidden histories, and fostering creativity through challenging conventional publishing wisdom with books and bookettes about DIY skills, food, bicycling, gender, self-care, and social justice. What was once a distro and record label was started by Joe Biel in his bedroom and has become among the oldest independent publishing houses in Portland, OR. We are a politically moderate, centrist publisher in a world that has inched to the right for the past 80 years.

Global labor conditions are bad, and our roots in industrial Cleveland in the 70s and 80s made us appreciate the need to treat workers right. Therefore, our books are MADE IN THE USA and printed on post-consumer paper.

Library of Congress Cataloging-in-Publication Data

Names: Blue, Elly, editor
Title: Biketopia : feminist bicycle science fiction stories in extreme
  futures / [edited by Elly Blue]
Description: Portland, OR : Elly Blue Publishing, [2017] | Series: Bikes in
  space ; 4
Identifiers: LCCN 2016035843 (print) | LCCN 2016057829 (ebook) | ISBN
  9781621062066 (pbk.) | ISBN 9781621069843 (epdf) | ISBN 9781621061939
  (epub) | ISBN 9781621064282 (mobi)
Subjects: LCSH: Science fiction, American. | Feminist fiction, American. |
  Cycling--Fiction.
Classification: LCC PS648.S3 B525 2017 (print) | LCC PS648.S3 (ebook) | DDC
  813/.0876208--dc23
LC record available at https://lccn.loc.gov/2016035843

[TABLE OF CONTENTS]

INTRODUCTION

The future isn't looking so good right now. That's the story we're increasingly telling ourselves anyway, and it's a story that the world's scientists can back up. So you open up a science fiction book to escape into a post-apocalyptic world where humans have either pulled it together or we haven't, where we're variously reaping the rewards or paying the price of survival. But at least it's a future with humans who have stories to tell.

And in this case, those stories all involve bicycles.

When it's good, science fiction is pretty much always a projection of the concerns of the present. And one of the main themes in the stories submitted to this volume was the potential dystopia contained within our present utopian fantasies of salvation from climate catastrophe. Can only totalitarian enforcement of drastic environmental measures preserve human life on the planet? If it all goes to shit, will we all end up fractured, stranded alone, and in squalor? Or will ongoing environmental catastrophe pave the way for even more dictatorship and destruction? Or will some of us be fine or more than fine while the rest are horrifically left behind?

These are pretty dramatic questions, but you can hear them underneath everyday discussions about things like where to put a bike lane, if people with nowhere else to live should be allowed to camp near the bike path, or if it matters that everyone on the advisory committee is white. They're the questions lurking in the background as we neglect to plan for retirement or as we watch the approach of the next mega-storm that's supposed to come every 500 years and now turns up every three.

A smart person told me that the key to having a good life in the face of the world's uncertainty is to find something that is meaningful to you and go all-in for it. For me, that's the real appeal of both bicycles and science fiction—no matter how grim the world looks, each one can take you to a place where you can see other perspectives and explore your options with openness and creativity.

- *Elly Blue, Portland, Oregon*

RIDING IN PLACE

Sarena Ulibarri

Colette stared out at the blue rim of Earth as she pedaled the stationary bike. Only three more weeks. She missed the sun most of all, a fact she never would have admitted to her daughter, who had recently joined a sun goddess cult. Colette had fought against her joining, but being drafted to the asteroid mines made her authority evaporate. From orbit, the sun was nothing but a cold glare, when it was even visible. Without an atmosphere for it to shine through, it was just another star.

Someone else set up on the bike next to hers. Colette kept her gaze on the planet as the station's rotation slowly pulled it across the window. She pushed herself harder, aiming for that point of exertion where she felt as solid as she would on the ground with gravity pulling against her bones. If she pushed hard enough, it almost felt like the bike would actually take her somewhere. The wheels spun and the station spun as it hurled at a dizzying speed around the spinning Earth. So much rotation and revolution—but no forward motion, except for time. She peaked, slowed down, and fished her tube out of its pack for a drink of water. She closed her eyes, legs still pumping, but easing down.

"Dreaming about utopia?" the other person said.

Colette snorted. "I don't believe in utopia."

"Why not?"

"Because people live there." Colette opened her eyes and glanced at her conversation partner. "Oh, sorry," she said. "I didn't realize you were . . . you were . . ." She still wasn't sure about the right term for the AI workers that populated the mining stations along with the drafted human miners. "Robot" just seemed so crude.

The AI smiled kindly at Colette, a little crinkle at the corner of her eyes. She pedaled faster as Colette slowed down. The

AI workers were indistinguishable from humans except for their hairless heads and a pallid waxiness to their skin. That, of course, and the ability to turn their limbs instantly into whatever tool was needed, like walking Swiss army knives. Couple that with the fact that they didn't need space suits to go out onto the asteroid and Colette wondered why they even still bothered to draft humans into the mines. Surely it was the same people who decided that everyone needed to put in time at their local vertical farms. Know where your food comes from; know where your solar panels and circuit boards come from. It made sense from an ideological standpoint, but from a practical standpoint it ripped people out of their lives at inconvenient times.

"Yes," the AI said. "I can see why the presence of people would complicate perfection. Would you rather be *there*, though?" She gestured toward the Earth in the window.

"Oh, yes," Colette said. "Where I live, there are tree-lined bike paths you can ride through the whole city. The bike paths even spiral up the outsides of the buildings so you can ride all the way to the rooftop parks." Colette brought herself to a stop and stepped off the bike.

The AI nodded. "I would like to see that someday."

Colette toweled off and left the gym with a casual, "See you later," and it wasn't until the door to her room slid open that the strangeness of the AI's words hit her. An AI worker wanted to visit Earth?

•   •   •

Another tedious week passed of hacking at ore seams and analyzing stone flakes. The asteroid looped the planet once every twenty-three hours, so the miners could still pretend at something like night and day if they wanted to. Colette saw the AI from the gym a few times, drifting through the Swiss cheese holes of the asteroid with nothing but a tether around her waist. The AIs slid through space like dolphins, while the humans maneuvered with all the grace of an elephant seal.

It was a week after their first encounter when Colette found the AI in the gym again, already spinning. Colette draped her towel over the handlebars and climbed on.

"I thought AIs didn't need exercise," she said.

"We don't," the AI said. "But humans do plenty of things they don't need to do, too."

"True enough," Colette said. She eased into her pedaling, wincing at the weakness in her legs. "We sure need *this*, though. I'm surprised this place isn't packed all the time."

In fact, all the other bikes were empty. Humans were supposed to visit the gym daily to maintain bone density, but no one enforced the rule. Colette would have been here whether she was supposed to or not. In two more weeks, she would feel the wind on her face as she rode.

"What's your name?" Colette asked.

"Eight Ten," the AI answered.

"You don't have a . . . casual name? Like something you're called by your, er, robot friends?" Colette looked away in embarrassment, pedaled harder. The miners' training covered the geology and chemistry of the asteroid, how to work around explosives, and how to limit the negative effects of space on the human body. It covered everything except for how to talk to a robot.

"It begins to sound like a name if you say it often enough."

"Eight Ten," Colette tried out. "Sure."

It didn't sound like a name. It sounded like one of the group monikers the members of her daughter's sun goddess cult took on when they joined, when they attempted to abandon their individuality, speaking only as "we" instead of "I." Her daughter had stopped answering to "Marisol" several months before Colette was drafted, and it drove Colette crazy.

"What's your favorite place on Earth?" Eight Ten asked.

Colette laughed. "I haven't seen the whole planet."

"Of what you have seen, then."

She thought about it. Her heartbeat thudded in her ears. She took a deep breath and tried to maintain her pace on the bike. Her legs burned.

"Probably the stained glass gardens," she answered finally. "I don't remember what they're actually called. It's like a long, snake-shaped greenhouse. Several miles of dirt path with plants all along the side. The walls and ceiling are bright stained glass with portraits of birds, like parrots or owls. They're all made of solar panels, of course."

"Of course," Eight Ten echoed.

Everything was made of solar panels. They were in their windows, in their clothes, in their sidewalks. Earth brimmed with the sun's energy, overflowing even into the dark or rainy corners. That's why the miners were here—a world so dependent on silicon had threatened to turn Earth's deserts into endless sandpits until they managed to lasso some asteroids into orbit. Now deserts could be restored like the rest of the healing planet, and the world's glass and gold came straight from the stars.

"I used to take my daughter there," Colette said.

"These are not happy memories?" Eight Ten must have picked up on the tone of Colette's voice.

"They are. But we've had differences since. I don't like the sun goddess cult she joined. She doesn't like me calling it a cult."

"No utopia where there are disobedient daughters," Eight Ten said.

Colette finished her bike ride in silence. She tried to think about the stained glass gardens, about the feel of the sun on her back as she rode through the city, but all she could manage to remember were the days when it got so hot that everything shut down because it was dangerous to go outside. It had been one of those shut-in days that Marisol had first announced her intention to join the sun goddess cult.

Colette puffed her way through her final mile. Two more weeks.

•   •   •

"The AIs have never left the station, have they?" Colette asked the doctor who examined her for the start of out-processing. One more week until she headed back to Earth. For good, if she was lucky. She'd seen Eight Ten in the gym several more times, and each time the AI had asked her to describe something about Earth.

"No," the doctor said. "They were constructed here on the station."

"And when they die?"

"Well, they don't really die, but if they cease functioning, they can be recycled." She tapped in a few notes and then told Colette, "You should have minimal negative effects once you return to Earth. Just keep doing what you're doing for the next week and you should be fine."

Colette stared at her own hands. "Recycled."

"Ah," the doctor said. "Yes, it's common to empathize with the AIs when you haven't been around them very long. But think about it this way. If their parts get disassembled and recycled into a different machine, is that really any different than an organic body being decomposed and reused by Earth?"

"Is that supposed to be comforting?"

The doctor shrugged. "I know they seem very alive. But they aren't really human."

Colette looked up at her. "Humans have a long history of claiming certain people aren't really human."

She frowned. "It truly is different."

"Maybe," Colette said. "Maybe."

• • •

"Why do you want to visit Earth?" Colette asked before she even stepped onto the bike.

Eight Ten pedaled steadily. "It sounds beautiful."

"You can get the same effect from the station gardens," Colette said, but she knew it wasn't true. The gardens were nice, but it was nothing like walking through a city arboretum, much less a real forest or jungle. Three more days.

"I don't want to live there," Eight Ten said. "I just want to visit it. Walk around. See the utopia we helped create."

"It's not a utopia," Colette said, almost automatically. But she thought she understood. Human workers were sent to the asteroid mines so they could see the source of their abundant energy, understand the work and struggle behind their everyday conveniences. Why then shouldn't the AI workers be given a chance to see the benefits of *their* hard work?

They pedaled in silence, just the whoosh of the wheels, the puff of Colette's breathing. Today she really felt like she was getting nowhere, riding in place. Three more days and she could ride all the way across the city. Out into the forests, if she wanted to. After a moment, she glanced over at Eight Ten.

"Have you asked the supervisors to let you go down with one of the shuttles?"

"Yes."

"What did they say?"

Eight Ten abruptly stopped pedaling and stepped off the bike. "They said that I was a machine, so I did not know what I wanted."

• • •

The next day, in the middle of a shift change, the alarms went off. Alarm protocol was like the exercise regime; everyone was supposed to have learned and practiced it, but most people hadn't. The AIs retreated calmly to their docking stations while the humans shouted and ran like the scared animals they were. Lights flashed and sirens blared. Jumbled announcements ordered people to the shuttle bay.

Colette, just off her shift, struggled out of her spacesuit and hurried in that direction. She felt both terrified and elated. Alarms meant danger, but an evacuation meant her last two days had shrunk to zero.

Shuttles popped off and tumbled toward the planet. Bodies surged into the few remaining ones, sorting into seats. Colette kept pushing toward empty seats just before they were filled. She looked around for a vacant spot and did a double-take at one of the women who was strapping her seatbelt on.

It was Eight Ten, wearing a tight, brown wig, makeup smeared on her face to hide her waxy skin. Eight Ten recognized Colette as well. The AI's eyes pleaded with her.

"No more room!" someone shouted. "Everyone not strapped in needs to get out and find a different shuttle."

Colette took a step toward Eight Ten and then paused, the words that would betray the AI's presence stuck in her throat.

"Out! Out!" several people yelled. Colette hesitated a moment longer, then stepped out of the shuttle.

The hatch sealed and the shuttle took off. The alarms still blared. Colette ran to check the other shuttles but they had all dropped. She and a dozen or so other humans lingered, mostly supervisors and rotational engineers who seemed resigned to having been left behind. Why did they not have enough shuttles for everyone? No one, human or AI, should have to go down with the ship.

Colette walked slowly back to the gym. It still had the best view of Earth she'd found on the station, but it wasn't in sight just now. Had Eight Ten tripped the alarms so she could escape during the chaos? Or had she taken advantage of a real alarm? At this point, it didn't really matter. Colette had given up her place. There was no reversing the shuttle drops. She touched the general use screen just inside the door, entered her worker ID, and then called her daughter. To her surprise, she answered, though the image was unsteady, as though she were walking somewhere.

"Is everything sunny?" Marisol asked. "We just got the emergency alert."

That "we" grated at Colette even now. "I didn't know you got those alerts."

"Of course we do. What's going on?"

Colette shook her head. "I don't know. But the shuttles are gone."

Her daughter stopped walking and her face centered in the screen. "Gone?"

"Listen, Marisol, I need you to do something for me. Please. The shuttles will land in about an hour. There's an AI on one of them and she needs protection. See if the Sisters of the Sun can help her. Don't let them send her back right away. Don't let her get recycled or imprisoned. Please. It's important to me." No matter the truth, Colette wanted her sacrifice to have been worth it, for the AI to see the Earth she so desperately wanted to see.

Marisol squinted, her eyes tracking back and forth as she processed the request. "Okay," she finally said, the syllables full of surprise and determination. "Okay, we can do that."

"I have to go." Colette's head ached from the continued scream of the alarms. She reached to turn off the screen.

"Mom," Marisol said. Colette paused. "I hope everything is okay on the station."

And the screen went black. Colette shut her eyes. That was probably the closest she was going to get. Marisol had said "I" rather than "we," which was a small victory. And Colette had called her daughter's group by its name, the Sisters of the Sun, rather than "the sun goddess cult." Compromise. It wasn't so bad.

She placed her hands on the handlebars, mounted the bike, and rode in place. She stared through the window, waiting for the blue rim of the planet to appear.

Maybe Earth was a utopia, of a sort, after all. Maybe the scorching days, the devastating storms, the family battles, the political meddling, maybe all of those were part of that utopia. Because, she thought as she pedaled, people couldn't just bike in place and be happy. They needed to ride over hills, around corners. They needed obstacles; they needed to push themselves, to make it to the finish line before the person next to them. They needed to look back at the path they'd ridden and know that they'd gotten somewhere.

Earth peeked over the windowsill and the alarms silenced. Someone passed by the open gym door, telling someone else, "False alarm, something weird in the circuits."

Colette let out a long breath of relief. She pictured Eight Ten, her robotic arms transformed into tools, clandestinely manipulating some circuits to trigger the alarms.

Earth filled the window now. Two days, or maybe a little longer after all this, but soon, Colette would walk the planet's surface again. But today, as soon as the shuttle landed, Eight Ten would see her utopia for the first time.

TAMING THE BEAST

Robert Bose

I cried when they came for the Tesla. Sure she was vintage, and the battery wouldn't hold much of a charge, but I loved the old girl. The car had been the first major purchase of my life, a deep blue carbon fiber rocket to explore my tiny universe with. And explore I did. I'd even given her a name. Mavis. My friends had laughed when they found out. A low-tech car with a name? How quaint. They could see giving one to a fancy A.I., or maybe even an orbital shuttle, but antique autonomous transport vehicles only rated an alphanumeric sequence. The workers loaded Mavis onto a flatbed hover truck and sent her off to the great recycling centre in the sky, a victim of the long planned phase-out of personal vehicular traffic in the sprawling metropolis of Northern Heaven.

Her replacement arrived by mega-drone the next morning. An oversized crate emblazoned with a banner that read ZEN9. Below was printed "No Assembly Required," "Made from 100% Natural Graphene," and the standard "Failure to recycle all packing materials will result in a fine and re-education under ordinance 1138-B."

The matte black bicycle, once extricated, was sleek and sporty. It seemed to have everything—solid wheels with active suspension for an ultra smooth ride, a full electronics package, and most of all, a beautiful and comfortable seat. I wanted to like it. I really did. My mind screamed yes while my heart wavered, uncertain. Maybe I still mourned for Mabel, but the bike looked and felt more like a work of art than a potential companion. I could see the beast encased in glass, hanging on the wall in my apartment, with a plaque that read, "*Sabertooth*."

I'd debated, with my friends and myself, on whether I even needed a new commuting vehicle. I could walk. Many did. It was only an hour each way on the well-travelled and scenic path. Mass transit, on the other hand, was right out. The tube system was a frightening combination of zero personal space and the threat of resurgent retroviruses. One cough and everyone slapped on a hideous mask. Ugh. While most people didn't miss driving, I did. I loved the quick trip on empty roads, my favorite music blasting away, wrapped in a tranquil oasis of personal space.

I awoke the next morning in an apprehensive mood. The caffeinated corn flakes and synthetic milk sat heavy in my stomach. Maybe I should just walk, take advantage of an hour of fresh air. Yes. No. The bike sat there, taunting me. I was in excellent shape but hadn't ridden one since college. Did the stationary ones at the gym count? I debated in silence, stood in the hallway in my brand new kit, and stared at the machine.

"Sweet ride, Ish," said Dyson.

My next-door neighbor had snuck up on me while I deliberated. He was young and ultra-athletic. One of those peppy health club cultists with glowing skin, muscles on muscles, and a terrible fashion sense. Flip flops? In 2046? The way he ran his hands lovingly across the lacquered frame made me jealous.

"Thanks. Got it last night."

"Do you have a race planned?"

"Ha! No. I'm going to ride to work."

He gave me a funny look. "That's a lot of bike. It would be wasted as a commuter. You should race it."

"It's what they sent me in exchange for my car. Equivalent value."

"Ah. You read the manual and set the program up yet? The ZEN series takes a fair amount of configuration." He reached for the command bar.

I stepped between him and the bike. "Thanks. I got it."

He held up his hands. "Okay, okay, just trying to help. Good luck with it. I'll see you around."

"Later." He shook his head as he bounced down the hall. *Me, race?* The thought lingered in the back of my mind. Crazy.

I got to the path and watched the wave of professionals leaving the block. Workers of all genders streamed towards the creative district in a garish clash of scarlet and lavender, the dominant combination of the current season. Masks dangled from the necks of those headed to the tube.

Not me, though. With my black kit and blacker bike, I made my own fashion rules and I had to admit, we looked damned good together. Where the Tesla had been obsolete, the ZEN screamed cutting edge. Where the car had creaked with age and infirmities, the bike rolled with silent grace.

A perfect day. Engineered that way, sure, but still perfect. The light breeze smelled of chocolate and roasting coffee. The sun glinted through the dome, refracting at its extreme angle, tossing rainbows. I could have just stood there and enjoyed the view, but work wasn't going to wait and I'd wasted enough time.

Helmet. Goggles. I slipped onto the seat and clipped my feet into the pedals. The bike came to life on its own and adjusted to my size with a quiet whir. The control and sensor systems came online, the heads-up display listing them off one by one. "Lights. Signal Lights. Braking System. Proximity Alerts. Hive Mind Adaptive Cruise Control. Advanced Systems."

I set out down the path with a gentle ding in my ear and a pleasant female voice chirping, "Oncoming pedestrian," then, "Oncoming cyclist," and then, "Move to right, traveller passing on left." The notifications soon became tiresome.

"Bike, turn off the alerts."

Nothing.

"Bike. Turn off the warnings. Please."

Still nothing.

"Bike. Turn off the farking notifications or turn down the volume or something. Do you understand me?"

The constant barrage continued.

"Listen to me, you expensive piece of junk!"

I pressed the various buttons on the command bar without success. Maybe Dyson was right and I should have read the bloody manual. Screw it, I still could. I tapped my watch and initiated a network query.

"Question: How do you get a new ZEN9 to respond to verbal commands?"

"Answer: The bicycle should respond to directed guidance."

Wow, how utterly helpful.

"Question: What to do if a ZEN9 does not respond to directed guidance?"

"Answer: If the bicycle is malfunctioning, please make a maintenance appointment."

I took a deep breath. I'd have to suffer for another twenty minutes, but I could grit my teeth and try to ignore it.

The pathway merged into a primary commuter thoroughfare. The trickle of commuters became a fire hose—an immense crush of walkers, joggers, power boarders, blade runners, and fellow bikers. My head was ringing from the non-stop notifications, so when the navigational prompt gave me the option of switching to an actual road, I took it.

The expressway carried industrial transport drones, transit feeder busses, and a small number of personal vehicles yet to be decommissioned. The electric cars invoked jealousy. I'd taken Mabel down the route, four times a week, for the last six years. I knew it well. Every turn. Every landmark.

"Fark."

I didn't want to dwell on the past, even if it was only yesterday, so I got into the groove, hugged the shoulder, and reacted to a terrifying "Move to extreme right, extra-wide load passing on left" alert. I bounced around in the giant drone's wake and I heard what sounded like a swarm angry bees, not far behind, coming up fast.

"Bike, turn on the rear view camera."

No effect.

I grumbled and resorted to manual, you know, looking over my shoulder, as the fast moving sound swept up and overtook me in a garish blur of Teflon aero-gear and neon brand badges.

"On your left."

Sleek forms hugging mad racing bikes whirled over the fused plastic road surface. They reminded me of great cats on the hunt.

The ZEN9 spoke in a new voice. Hard. Humorless. "Compatible group located. Engaging Peloton Mode." It sounded almost sinister.

The bike reconfigured itself into a more streamlined shape, pushing me forward and down into an aggressive stance. Heart rate, power, and cadence joined the speed number on the display. Urging me to increase my velocity, tiny reticulating filaments snaked out of the top tube and into my thighs. Electrical jolts forced my quads to contract and my legs engaged without conscious control. I caught up with the pack five minutes later and my repeated exclamations of "Farking Piper" produced a few thumbs up.

Names and statistics flashed across my goggles. Amber, 121 BPM, 205 Watts, 82 RPM. Tasha, 124 BPM . . . and so on.

One bike slipped back alongside. A nod. "It's great to see some new blood on the road. Been riding long?"

"Not really." My voice cracked. I needed a drink. And a place to lie down and die.

"The name's Kira. Love the bike. You can't go wrong with a ZEN."

"Thanks. I'm Ishani." I huffed. "Mine seems to have a life of its own."

"Ha ha! Don't you know it. Zahara, up there at the front, has an 8. Had a bit of a rough go until she tamed it, but now it's amazing."

"What's the secret?"

She edged closer until our bikes were almost touching. "You need to find its name. Its true name."

A name. Of course! I tightened my fists on the handlebars. "Is there a trick to it? I've already called it a number of, uh, descriptors."

Kira smiled. "It'll come. You'll just have to tease it out."

"Thanks. I hope so. Are you a racing team? You seem so hardcore."

"Hardly. Just friends with common interests. We ride before work most weekdays and race each Sunday. You should join up and get to know everyone. We have a lot of fun."

"I might just do that."

"End of the line. Hope to see you around." The seven bikes split off in various directions.

"Peloton Mode disengaged." The cheery voice was back.

My impromptu adventure had taken me far from work. I circled a small urban farm while I reoriented. The mixture of adrenaline and endorphins faded but I knew I'd seize up if I stopped. A small girl picking berries waved every time I went around. Deep breaths. I needed the name. The true name.

The machine seemed so alive, so dynamic, a great feral beast with a mind of its own. I'd just been along for the ride while it prowled the urban jungle. Dierdre? Montsho? Tahki? No. I wasn't going to go down that road. Names were powerful and things became the personification of one's thoughts.

Then I had it. My first pet, the kitten my mother had given me on my first day of pre-school, the day that I'd been more afraid of than any other in my young life. The fierce little creature had gotten me through it, and more. She, too, had a mind of her own until we'd come to an *agreement* on who was the boss. "I'm going to call you Mabel."

There was a faint note, like the sound of angelic harps, and the computer spoke. "Name accepted. Peer to peer interaction enabled."

Finally! "Well, Mabel, great to know you. Now turn off every one of those blasted alerts."

"Non-critical proximity alerts disabled."

"And let's get the hell out of here. Second star to the right, and straight on 'til morning."

"Plotting most direct path."

"Excellent. We are going to get along just fine, you and I, just fine."

Twenty-five minutes, later I crawled into my office, a wasted shadow of my former self. I lay on the floor in an expanding pool of sweat and watched my legs spasm in an uncontrollable dance of rhythmic contortions. I could only think of one thing. Painkillers. Actually three things. Wine and chocolate. Okay, four things. Racing.

Bob, my creative partner, walked in and stroked his long, braided beard. "First day on a ZEN9? Management loves those." He sniffed. "I heard the shower's offline though."

MEET CUTE

Maddy Spencer

SIGNAL LOST

Gretchin Lair

A s Tara fumbled to silence her data device, one of the notifications snapped her awake:

- Congratulations! You're pregnant!

Tara sat up in bed and grinned. David was still asleep, but she couldn't resist a squeak of delight. She scrolled through all her health notifications:

- Today's NutriGoals
- Today's Activity Targets
- CareFull Insurance status changes
- CareFull Wellness Goals changes
- Your baby & you: Week 1
- [CAL] Prenatal appointment scheduled
- Pregnancy Exercise & Nutrition (PEN) enrollment
- Toys"R"Us® WellOne access request
- Babies"R"Us® WellOne access request
- Johnson & Johnson® WellOne access request

When she finally reached the pregnancy notification again, she eagerly scanned for details:

- Implantation confirmed at 2:34 a.m.
- Expected due date: 38 weeks, 3 days
- hCG levels: OK
- Fetal Development Score: 5/5

Unable to contain herself, she nudged David.

"What?" As he turned over, his device chimed too. He reached for it as he opened his eyes, but Tara quickly leaned over to take it from him.

"Wait, no! Don't look yet! Let me tell you!"

David blinked sleepily and rose on one elbow. "Tell me what?"

"We're pregnant!"

David smiled. "We're pregnant?"

"We're pregnant!" Tara cried, setting both devices on the bedside table before bouncing into his arms.

•   •   •

David cleaned up after breakfast. He scrolled through their shared health notifications to read the pregnancy notification again, smiling.

He heard three slow beeps from the garage as Tara got her bike ready for work. He cocked his head as he closed the dishwasher. Again, three slow beeps.

David's pulse quickened. After Tara's accident, they had agreed to share heartbeats so he wouldn't worry when she rode her bike. Usually it was a comfort, but sometimes it betrayed the fear he tried to hide.

"Everything okay in there, hon?" David asked, lightly.

Tara emerged, frowning. "It says 'Fetal Protection Mode Engaged.' It says I need a medical override."

"What?" David asked. "Let me see."

They stood by the bike and read the alert.

"Hmmm. Yeah. When's your prenatal appointment scheduled?"

"Not for three weeks!"

"Well, we can share a car," David suggested. "I scheduled one today. You can ride with me until you get to the doctor. Better safe than sorry."

He sounded a little more relieved than he probably should have and Tara stomped into the house.

•   •   •

Tara swept into the restaurant after work, glowing. She and David had been coming here since they moved in together. Don, the owner, always had a smile for them. The hosting screen beeped, and after a surprised look Don smiled even more widely. "Hey, congratulations on the baby!"

"Thank you!" Tara sang, practically skipping to her favorite booth where David waited. They held hands and beamed.

Don followed her over. "The usual?"

"Yes, please!" they said. Tara returned her attention to David. "I had such a good day today!" she gushed.

"Yeah, you seem pretty happy," he agreed. "I was worried you might still be mad about the car."

"Oh, no, the car was great! I still hate that 'Fetal Protection Mode Engaged' announcement, but I loved how it adjusted the seat and everything for me. Even the temperature!"

"Well, I'm glad you like it. You can ride with me as long as you want."

"Hey, guess what? Sarah said I'll get three extra personal days while I'm pregnant and automatic access to the nursing room."

"I thought you weren't going to tell anyone at work yet," David said. "Especially your boss."

"Yeah, I was kind of surprised too, but apparently HR updated my company profile. So Sarah had to tell me about some new benefits and stuff."

"I guess that makes sense," David replied. "Hey, where did you get those quotes you sent me today?"

"Oh, CareFull sent me \$10 off my first baby book download! It's worth 500 points towards our Wellness Goals discount. Speaking of which, did you notice my NutriGoals today?"

"I saw your ranking was higher than mine," David said, trying and failing to look upset.

"Ha! Yeah, when the cafeteria scanned my chip today I got a special 'fetal-friendly' menu, so I ordered the brown rice bowl. Isn't that great? When I do lunch with Jenny it always gives her the low-sodium options, but it's never actually happened to *me* before!"

"Well, then, it is truly a special day indeed," David teased. Tara rolled her eyes, but smiled.

Don returned, looking serious. "Sorry, I can't give you the tuna. What else can I get you?" He handed her a menu.

"What?" Tara said.

"Yeah, sorry. Because of the baby. No sake, either."

Crestfallen, Tara saw the fetal-friendly menu was missing many of her favorite items. "C'mon, Don. We're celebrating! Can't I have *any* sushi?"

Don shook his head. "My liability insurance would go through the roof. Health chip readers give me a big discount to avoid allergies and dietary restrictions." He pointed: "Look, the cucumber rolls are good."

David said, "Can *I* have the tuna?"

"Oh, yeah, sure," Don said.

Tara glared at David.

"Actually, the cucumber rolls will be fine," he said.

•　　　•　　　•

"Honestly, I'm surprised you still let her ride that bike after the accident," Cheryl said.

David coughed as he put down his beer. He studiously avoided looking at Tara, who tightly gripped her glass of sparkling water.

"Cheryl, seriously?" Ellen said. She turned to David. "Don't listen to her."

They sat together on Ellen's back porch on a cool spring night. Strings of light cast a warm glow on them while the rest of the party murmured inside, punctuated by laughter and music.

"He doesn't *let* me ride the bike," Tara said, each word crisp and piercing.

"I'm just saying," Cheryl said. "Now that you're having a baby, you need to be more careful."

"When you're the one having this baby, you can do it your way," Tara said hotly. "My fetal development score is 5/5, thank you very much."

Before the argument could escalate, Amy and Justin emerged from the house, holding their new baby. "Goodbye! Anna's ready to go home," Amy said. Justin beamed.

Anna's sleeping face immediately melted the tension and everyone gathered around the baby to whisper their goodbyes.

"She's so tiny!" Tara said.

"Yeah, she came early," Amy said, rubbing Anna's cheek. "Just couldn't wait to join us, I guess!"

Justin said, "Amy had gestational diabetes. We didn't catch it early enough."

"Yeah, next time I'm totally going to have to get a chip," Amy said, rocking back and forth.

"You didn't have a chip?" Tara said.

Amy smiled ruefully. "No. I hate those things. I hate that insurance companies make us get them."

Justin said, "They don't *make* us."

Amy said, "No, but we had to pay a penalty for not having one."

"We lost the incentive," Justin said.

"Same thing," Amy said mildly, rolling her eyes. It was obviously an argument they had had before. "But now that I'm 'high risk' I pretty much have to get one."

Cheryl said, "But if it can catch something that goes wrong . . . Better safe than sorry."

Everyone nodded.

"Yeah, I know," Amy said. "But they mostly want the health data. Especially the pregnancy data. I hate all those alerts and updates and spam, but if I want to keep my health insurance, I gotta use the chip."

Anna shifted in her sleep, so Amy and Justin whisked her off. As they left, Tara's device offered her a progress update:

- Activity Targets: 3/5 stars
- NutriGoals: 4/5 stars
- Low on Vitamin E: eat foods like almonds, spinach, and kale to boost your Vitamin E levels!
- Fetal Development Score: 4/5

Tara's heart sank. She locked eyes with David and knew he had seen the fetal development score dip, too.

• • •

"I wouldn't worry about it," Dr. Coleman said, smiling as if she had been asked this question many times. She was visibly pregnant, her white coat unable to close over her belly.

Tara sat on the edge of her seat. "But what am I doing wrong? I'm trying to do everything right!"

"The FDS is pretty loose. I wouldn't worry about it until it dips to two or three, and even then only if it lasts a couple of days."

"Then why do they even *have* the other numbers? I thought it was important to come to the doctor if anything changed!"

Dr. Coleman sighed a little, her smile slipping. "Lots of things can affect your FDS from day-to-day, like sleep, stress, water intake, that kind of thing. And anyone can add additional limits. Like, I don't mind if you use the occasional Advil while you're pregnant, but WellOne had a medical consultant or a lawyer who did, so—"

"But I didn't take any Advil!"

Dr. Coleman waved her hand. "That's just an example. They must not have had any pregnant women involved in the FDS, or they would have known it drives us crazy. But really, it's nothing to worry about."

The doctor spun her chair towards her screen and tapped some boxes Tara couldn't see. "Okay, now let's look at that bike override. It's great you want to be active, we just want you to be careful. That accident you had a couple of years ago places you in a high-risk category, so you'll still get a warning whenever you use the bike, but it will go away after a few minutes. If your heart rate goes over 130, you'll get another warning. I'll download the data from your chip and your bike every week to make sure everything is going smoothly. If I notice any balance issues, I'll put another override on the bike. But otherwise I'll see you at your 16-week checkup!"

•   •   •

On the first sunny day in weeks, Tara sat sobbing on the curb outside the market, waiting for David to arrive. Her bike lay next to her.

"I came as soon as I saw the alert," David said. "What's wrong? Were you in an accident?"

Tara cried, "They won't let me buy lunchmeat! Or cheese! Or *yogurt*!"

David blinked. "Yogurt? But I thought that was good for you!"

"So did I! But I guess some new rule was passed? They weren't really sure, they just said I'd have to call my insurance company. Who makes these rules, anyway? Have any of them actually *been* pregnant?"

He sat down and wrapped his arm around her. She rested her head on her knees.

"I can't do this anymore," she said, slightly muffled. "I'm going to deactivate the chip tomorrow."

"What? No, I know this is hard but—"

Her head snapped up. "It's not hard for *you*! They'll let *you* buy yogurt!"

"But—"

"I didn't even want this stupid chip! I just got it for the insurance discount!"

Their devices simultaneously sounded:

- Cortisol levels elevated

- Heart rate warning

- Dehydration alert

Tara snarled and jerked back, but before she could throw her device, David gently took it from her. "Look, stay here," he said. "I'll get you some yogurt, OK?"

Tara nodded, lips still pursed. "OK. Strawberry."

When David returned with a cup of yogurt and a plastic spoon, Tara was staring blankly at the parking lot. She didn't say anything as she peeled back the foil and stirred. After a few bites she said, "Thanks. I was seriously considering shoplifting."

David smiled weakly.

"I just don't understand what I'm supposed to do," Tara said. "How can I make my NutriGoals if I can't eat anything?"

"That doesn't mean you have to deactivate the chip, though. Can't you just ask your doctor for diet recommendations?"

Tara sighed and set the empty cup down. "It's not just that, David. It's everything. I feel like I'm under a microscope all the time. There are so many rules, and they're always changing, and I guess it all makes sense individually but all together it's like I'm suffocating. What if they take away my bike again? What if they decide I can't wear boots for some reason? I want to do the right thing, but I can't ever make my own damn decisions! And I feel like I'm a bad person to even *want* to."

She looked away. "And it's work, too. The copier won't let me make copies because the toner might hurt the baby. And . . . you know that conference I was going to? Apparently airlines won't let you buy tickets after twenty weeks if you've got an active chip. So my boss reassigned that whole project to someone else. I've been working on that project for six months! Nobody knows that project better than me!"

David deflated. "Oh, shit, Tara."

They sat in silence on the curb for a while, their heartbeats slowing and synchronizing. Shoppers entering the market glanced at them curiously.

David took a breath. "Look, I understand. But. If your health chip hadn't triggered the emergency alert when that guy hit you . . ." He traced a scar on her arm. "I can't lose you, Tara. I can't." He smiled a little. "Especially while we're pregnant."

Tara stood up abruptly and grabbed her bike. "*We're* not pregnant. Don't ever say that again."

•　　　•　　　•

Dr. Coleman laughed. "If you think it's bad now, wait until you have the baby!" She patted her belly.

Tara persisted. "Seriously. This chip is stressing me out. I just want to deactivate it until after the baby."

"Tara, I don't think that's a good idea. Don't you want a healthy baby?"

Tara tried to keep her voice level. "Of course I want a healthy baby. But lots of women without chips still have healthy babies. I can follow the guidelines without the chip."

"Oh, but that's why health chip protocols are so useful," Dr. Coleman said. "They adopt guidelines from all kinds of places, like the World Health Organization, the American Medical Association, the California Office for Health Hazard Assessment—"

Tara's voice rose. "Exactly! There's so much advice and it's all contradictory! I get alerts all the time! It's driving me crazy!"

Dr. Coleman sat back in her chair and shrugged apologetically. "Actually, now that you're pregnant, I can't deactivate your chip."

Tara's eyes widened. "What do you mean? Like, it's illegal?"

"Oh, no, of course not," Dr. Coleman said, waving her hands and smiling. "But your insurance won't reimburse for it. And if I did it, my malpractice insurance would skyrocket. And there's also a big national initiative to reduce fetal complications, so the ethics committee at my affiliate hospital would rule against it."

Tara sat, stunned. "So what do I do?"

Dr. Coleman frowned. "Well, if you're really serious about this, I guess you could transfer your data to an IDC. But I don't recommend it. It's a big pain for everyone. Your insurance will reimburse at a different rate. You'd have to come in more often. And the data download is a lot slower."

She gestured towards her screen. It had a picture of her kids on it: a tow-headed boy looking offscreen and a tween girl with sharp knees and a big smile. "Most women really want the security a health chip provides during pregnancy. I know I did. I didn't have a chip when I had my daughter, but I did with my son. It seems hard now, but it's only a few months out of your life. I think you'll be glad you kept it."

Tara left the office to find David flipping through a WellOne health chip brochure in the waiting room. The family on the cover looked so happy.

"Are you off the grid now?" David asked. "I can still feel your heartbeat."

Tara shook her head, her voice stretched thin. "She won't deactivate it now that I'm pregnant."

David frowned. "She won't—but that makes it sound like a parole chip." He tried to laugh.

"Exactly," Tara said, walking out the door.

•   •   •

It was twilight when David stopped to grab a sweater from the bedroom. He was reaching to turn on the light when he heard a rustle from the bed.

"No, don't." Tara's voice was thick and heavy from crying.

"I thought you were downstairs. What's wrong?" He cautiously sat on the edge of the bed.

Tara rolled away from him. "I hate this, David. This should be a happy time for us, but every day I wake up and think 'What's it going to be today? How am I going to fail today? What's going to be wrong today? What won't I be able to do today?'"

David put his hand on her leg. He couldn't see her face but he could feel her tension.

"Don't drink! Don't smoke! Don't lift anything! Take your vitamins! Don't eat fish or cheese or eggs! Don't drink coffee!

Don't dye your hair! Don't work too hard! Don't bike too much! Be perfect!" She paused to take a breath. "I can't be perfect all the time!"

"Things will get better after the baby's born. I'll let you ride—"

Tara abruptly turned over and raised herself on one elbow. "You'll *what*? You'll *let me*? Is this still about the accident? You knew I rode a bike when you met me! You bought me that bike for Christmas!"

"I just want you to be safe, Tara! Especially now that we— you're pregnant."

"I gave you access to my heartbeat. What more do you want? Do I have to give up everything? Why does everyone get to control my life except me?"

"We only want what's best for you!" David said, hating how it sounded as he said it. He softened his tone: "It's not forever."

"Don't you get it?" Tara said. "This is just the start! There are going to be a million ways to get it wrong after the baby's born! And absolutely none of this is going to affect *you*."

"How can you say that?" David surprised himself with the force of his reaction. "Of course it will affect me! It already has! You think I like seeing you so unhappy? But I know how fast things can go wrong, Tara. You don't understand how scared I was! You almost died!"

Their devices dinged.

"But I *didn't* die, David! I'm still alive! We can't keep living as if I'm already dead! But I feel like I *am* dying with this chip." Tara's voice cracked. "I'm going to die if I have to keep doing this."

David climbed into bed and held her. Tara tensed, then gradually relaxed. Her tears were hot on his shoulder as they lay together in silence. Even without his device, he felt her heartbeat slowing as she fell asleep in his arms. But David stayed awake, staring into the dark for a long, long time.

•   •   •

Tara and David held hands as they waited in the Rebelle Collective office. The poster on the wall read, "It's *your* data. Let's keep it that way!"

A trim woman with short brown hair entered the room. She smiled and introduced herself as Karen, their health data coordinator. She held up a tablet and said, "I'm sorry, but first I have to read you this completely bullshit statement." She set her mouth in a grim line, reading quickly:

"This disclosure is required at the time of your initial consultation to ensure your voluntary and informed consent to transfer your data to an Independent Data Collective (IDC). You have the right to contact the State Department of Data Regulation to learn more about this IDC, including any relevant fine, penalty, or judgment rendered against this IDC or a data coordinator who provides services at this IDC."

Karen continued to read the disclosure before ending with: "You are not required to use an IDC. Using an IDC may place your data at higher risk and create unnecessary barriers to access. You may transfer your data from this IDC to another Data Collection Service (DCS) at any time."

"Wow," Tara said. "They really don't want you to transfer, do they?"

Karen smiled sadly. "Sorry. The big data collection services lobbied for that statement. Now they want to pass a three-day waiting period before you're even allowed to transfer to an IDC."

Tara shuddered, but plowed forward. "I can't find anyone to deactivate my chip. But David did some research and it looks like if I switch to Rebelle at least the health chip readers won't be able to see it, right?"

Karen nodded. "Well, with Rebelle you'll get to choose when to broadcast your data to health chip readers and what kinds of data you share with marketers. So you still get credit for having a chip, and it still collects data, but it's working *for* you, not *against* you."

Karen checked her tablet. "You're in week 11?"

Tara nodded.

"The end of the first trimester is a great time to transfer." Karen smiled. "Trust me, it gets even worse later. I used a big data collection service with my first kid and thought 'Never again!'"

David said, "I didn't even know you could change your data service until this happened. But it looks like most IDCs are really specialized. Like, Rebelle is just for pregnant women, right?"

"Yes, but by 'pregnant' we mean any woman who is, was, or wants to become pregnant. And their families too, of course. So that covers a lot! Will you be switching to Rebelle, too?"

David shook his head. "We'll lose our insurance discount if we both stop using our default data service."

Karen leaned forward slightly. "So then it's important to tell you that your insurance considers us to be an out-of-network data service, which means Tara won't be able to share data with you at all."

David sucked his breath through his teeth. "You mean, like . . . location data? And emergency alerts?" Tara felt David's heartbeat begin to race.

Karen nodded sympathetically. "Yeah. The health chip protocol carries a bunch of data it wasn't originally meant to. Are you sharing fetal updates?"

They nodded.

Karen made a pained face. "Ah. Then you won't get those notifications either, because they'll be part of her data, not yours."

"Oh," David said, crestfallen.

Tara's shoulders slumped. "Why do they make it so hard?"

Karen said, "I know. I'm sorry. A lot of people feel a little lost when they first transition to an IDC. If you're interested, we offer support groups and some handouts for mixed-data families."

"Yeah," David said. "This whole thing is turning out to be more complicated than I expected."

"Tell me about it," Tara said.

Karen tapped some things on her tablet and turned it towards Tara. "Still want to do this?"

Tara felt David's heartbeat pounding and squeezed his hand. She nodded briefly.

"OK, then." Karen passed the tablet over to her. "Place your thumb here to sign, please."

As soon as Tara touched the screen, David's heartbeat disappeared. Simultaneously, David's device barked in alarm. "Tara Robinson: Signal Lost."

David released a long shaky breath. "So that's it, huh?"

Karen nodded. "Well, it will take up to 48 hours for the health records to propagate. Location data goes immediately and credit scores are generally last. So if you're planning on buying a house, you should do that this weekend." She smiled a little at her own joke.

Tara reached for David's hand again. "Are you OK?"

"Yeah." David turned to face her. "But I'm going to miss you. And the baby."

"We're going to miss you, too," Tara said, tears rising.

David smiled faintly. "I know. But I want this to be a happy time for us, too."

Tara's device peeped. David's device remained silent. "Look," she said, showing him the notification. "At least we're still pregnant. 5/5."

"We're still pregnant?" David said uncertainly.

Tara smiled for the first time in months. "Yeah. We are."

PORTLANDTOWN

Elly Blue

Afeint to the left, a jab under the chin, a swing of the staff, followed by a crunch, a crumple, a crash—her foe staggered to the left and fell limp to the ground, landing sprawled across one of the others, a pile of pink and grey rags.

Mayana swung her staff back into ready position, scanning the woods for more encroaching enemies. She felt most alive in these moments after a battle. Her blood was up, time was slow, her senses were in perfect tune with the world around her, and a deep feeling of peacefulness flowed around her.

Birds. The spring sun weakly shining through budding branches of the young wood. Fresh earth, fresh death. She'd killed six guards, she saw, slowly turning in a circle. They were all very young, just children, really. Their uniforms were in terrible shape. How long had it been since the ornate leather armor of the Cascadian Republic had been bright and well cared for? Many seasons. And these Guards were scrawny. There hadn't been a lot of fight in them. Mayana had come to peace with bloodshed long ago, but these recent skirmishes troubled her deeply.

There might have been one or two more guards who'd gotten away. Well, she had no need to stay here long. This large of a patrol shouldn't have been out so early in the season. Had they gotten wind of the planned raid on the parts manufacturer? She needed to report back to Edgefield.

She snapped the staff back into its holster and went off in search of her bicycle.

It was a shame that the Reform hadn't kept up the old civil wars-era treaties, she thought, finding her rusty old bike in a thicket of ferns. It must have rolled there after she'd leapt off it, already taking her first swipe at the first guard, the one she hadn't seen in time and had nearly run over. She remembered the days of the last shaky accord that had allowed the Edgefield community to trade with what was now Portlandtown for food for industrial products and parts. It was three decades since the Leaders had come to power and decided that they would prefer swallow her people and their farms into the great industrial project of the Reformation. Her bicycle was even older than that. She was starting to feel her age, too—eyes dimmer, back stiffer, reactions slightly less lightning-quick than she expected to be. Still, she had all her parts and senses, and was in far better shape than she would have been living in the conditions of those pitiful child soldiers.

She swung her leg over the back of the bicycle, spun the pedal backward with her left foot, and stepped on—and then off again with a lurch, as the bike rolled a half turn and came to a sudden stop. She dismounted and crouched down to look.

Her chain had fallen from the sprocket and become fully wedged in between the gears and the frame. She pulled and pushed with her adjustable wrench. She broke off a branch and used it as a lever against the bike frame. Nothing. She rocked back on her heels and chewed the end of the branch, contemplating the bike. She'd need a better set of tools to dismantle the bike to free the chain, and those were all back at Edgefield. She laughed at herself. She'd just been gloating about her freedom from industrial indenture, and here she was stranded because she couldn't maintain her bicycle. An awkward position, which she would fight to hold until her last breath.

Mayana looked at the grey horizon. A few hours were left until sunset. If she set off now and was reasonably cautious, she could be back in home territory shortly after dark.

She shouldered her bike and started back.

•   •   •

Ko collapsed against the crumbling side of the overturned truck, her whole body heaving. She didn't know how many times she'd fallen in the undergrowth, tripping over bushes and hidden chunks of old, broken concrete. Her armor, battered enough when she had bravely put it on for the first time this morning, was now in tatters. Had she run far enough? Was the bloodthirsty anarchist still chasing her? She didn't know, but she had a terrible stitch in her side. She pressed herself hard against the truck, wishing she could disappear into it, or that another patrol from the town would come to rescue her. She couldn't see the sun, wasn't sure if she would know how to follow it home anyway. *What a disaster I am. What shame I've created for my mothers and sisters. My first day on duty and I run away from the fight where my comrades are being slaughtered. I let down the great Peace. I don't deserve to be rescued. I deserve to be beaten in Pioneer Square.* She could see it so clearly behind her clenched eyes—the trial, her penitence, the price she would pay, the scorn in her mother's eyes. Her mother's mother had sacrificed herself bravely for freedom in the Battle of Pendleton and Ko had always been expected to follow in her footsteps.

And then she heard it... actual footsteps. Her breath stopped short. She peeked around the side of the rock. It was the anarchist woman! And she was walking straight toward Ko, eyes locked on her. There was no hiding now, but Ko gasped and pulled her head back behind the rock anyway. She knew she should reach for her weapon and die fighting. Instead, she hugged her knees to her chest, squeezed her eyes shut, and listened to her pounding heart, waiting for the final blow of that staff to send her into oblivion. Nothing would be worse than returning to Portlandtown a coward. Nothing, she thought, hating herself even more for the disloyal thought, would be worse than returning there at all, constantly competing for food and small favors. Death, now that it was upon her, suddenly seemed like a wonderful option, and she felt her body relax.

But the blow never came.

Just, after what could have been seconds or hours, the sound of low, slow laughter.

Ko opened her eyes narrowly and saw bare feet and neatly patched brown cloth trousers. She raised her head to the anarchist's face. She was amazed to see a shock of gray hair, wrinkles around the eyes. The anarchist was smiling. No, she was laughing. Ko stared in amazement, disgust edging in on her shock and fear. Of course, the anarchists were all laughing at the townfolk. Mocking *us*. Everyone knew that.

"Hungry, little soldier?" the anarchist asked. She was holding something out toward Ko.

I should at least try to kill her, Ko thought. *So when they find me there'll be signs of a fight, so my sisters can see that I did my part to defend order and civilization from the ones who want to take it away from us.* But she became suddenly conscious of the longstanding ache in her belly. The hunger won out. She opened her hand, and the anarchist squatted down and put a piece of dry, hard biscuit into it. Ko devoured it. She expected bitter blandness, but it had an overpowering, strange flavor. Had the anarchist poisoned her? *Just as well*, she thought, and kept eating. But no, it was herbs for flavor, she remembered this taste from childhood. The food was waking her mind up, and she could breathe again.

The anarchist was still squatting just out of arm's reach, watching her eat. "There's better food back at Edgefield, and plenty of it," she said. "Why don't you come there with me?" Heat rushed to Ko's limbs while cold terror clenched her guts. She had never wanted anything more or felt such intense fear.

The anarchist chuckled again. "If I wanted to kill you, little soldier, I'd already have done it." She paused, thinking. "Let's make a bargain. If you don't attack me, I won't attack you. That's how we do things here outside the town, and most of the time it works pretty well. Cool?"

Ko found herself staring, frozen, and nodded.

The anarchist rocked back on her heels, still looking at her. She stuck out her hand again, this time without food in it. "I'm Mayana. Do you have a name?"

Ko just stared.

"It's alright. If you're coming with me, we need to start walking now. It's going to be much slower going after dark, which is coming up in about ..." she squinted upward "... just a couple hours now." She jumped up and offered Ko her hands.

Ko ignored them, scrambled to her feet unassisted. "My condition for joining you is a fair trial," she said, impressed at the steadiness in her own voice.

She was gratified to see a momentary expression of surprise on the anarchist's face before it evened out into steady bemusement again.

"A trial. For what crime?"

"I — " Ko stopped short, realizing she was in danger of incriminating herself. *Anything you say can and will be used against you* was the phrase they'd memorized in school, in the criminal justice unit. She mentally thanked the Reform Leaders for her education.

"I think you'll find we do things a little differently outside the city," the anarchist said, almost gently. "For now, we need to walk and we need to go quietly. When we are back at home base, I will answer all your questions. I can promise that you will be treated with respect, your needs will be met, and nobody will intentionally hurt you."

She turned away and walked quickly toward the edge of the clearing. Ko followed. But instead of striking off into the wood, the anarchist began pulling fern fronds aside and half-crawled under a bush, pulling out the rustiest bicycle Ko had ever seen. The anarchist picked it up and put it on her shoulder and started to walk.

Ko stood stock still, then ran to catch up. "Excuse me," she said, "Why don't you ride?"

The anarchist pointed to the chain lodged between the gears and the frame.

"Is that all?" Ko asked in amazement. "I can fix that in less than a minute."

"With the right tools," the anarchist pointed out.

Ko reached into her vest pocket and pulled out her standard issue pocket toolkit, emblazoned with the Reformation logo. "No problem."

Two hours later, they pulled up to what looked in the twilight like a thicket of bushes but what turned out to be the first checkpoint outside of Edgefield. Mayana, sitting sideways on the top tube, braked, and Ko, who had been taking a turn pedaling, hopped off the seat.

"Another defector?" said the guard, with a smile.

The word, its meaning, its application to her, didn't take root until they were pedaling again. She wanted to cry out, jump off the bike, and run back home. *But to what*, she thought. *And from what?* She had just seen her fellow recruits die violently, and now she'd thrown her lot in with their killer. It was too much to bear thinking about. The rhythmic motion of her legs, the bumpy forest path, the trees and bushes and clearings and rock formations passing by soothed her. She felt, in bursts, the hot shame for having run from the fight mixed with the terror of what she'd run from, the image of her flinching penitence in Pioneer Square, the image of her mother screaming with pain watching her daughter be beaten by fellow Guardians. And then, briefly overriding that shame, a feeling of peace. "Nobody will intentionally hurt you," the anarchist had said. Every time the shame and fear returned, those words came back too, and soothed them.

Ko kept pedaling, hands grasping the anarchist's waist, feeling grim. Regardless of everything, if those words were just the smallest bit true, Ko felt ready to gamble everything on them. For the first time in her life, she started to feel what real courage must be like.

•　　•　　•

All Chion had ever wanted was to be a Leader. From the moment when she was four years old and the Reformation Committee had first come on television with their announcement of peace and renewal, the path had been wide and clear before her.

She and her mother had made a sign that said "PEACE NOW" in bold, black letters, with a collage of images that Chion had cut from magazines—smiling children, food, and flowers, with factories in the background. Her mother had lifted her to the back of her bicycle, and they'd pedaled downtown to hold up the sign while the Reformers rolled into town in their tanks and armored vehicles. They'd done the same during the Reformation Parade each year, with Chion's signs getting better and better.

School had been easy for her, because she had a goal. She needed math so that she could manage Portlandtown's budget, science to hone her problem-solving skills, history so she could better understand the glorious role of her generation in the betterment of humanity. Civics class increased her resolve to serve, confirming the womanist pride she'd already learned at her mother's knee. Most important, sitting in that classroom had taught her to see who her friends and allies were, who was nodding off, and who was asking rebellious questions and would need to be watched later on.

As a teen, she'd founded the Young Leaders chapter of her high school and led it for four years. After high school, she had signed up for the community college communications program but gone and reported instead to Portlandtown Reformation Headquarters in the old City Hall. She'd known she had much more to learn before she was ready to lead. But a youthful heartbreak had swayed her into an emotional decision, for the first and she hoped last time in her life. It hadn't been a wrong decision, though. Looking back, she shuddered at the vision of stagnating in a classroom while the opportunities to actually do what she was learning were passing her by, or worse, going to classmates like Emily Hillhammer and LaShonda Adams.

She needn't have worried. She smiled, sitting at her desk and letting her mind drift while rubberstamping her signature on the morning's documents. LaShonda had been easy enough to deal with; Chion had had a word with one of her mother's friends to help her secure a training spot in the Diplomatic Evangelical corps. She now lived a rather swashbuckling life, leading long, dangerous missions around Cascadia, expanding and strengthening the boundaries of the Reformation and enjoying well-deserved glory in between. And Emily, who had worked summers at the crèche, had taken care of herself by setting her ambitions on leadership within the childcare and education system. No matter how high she might rise, Chion could not see a path for her to cross over into political leadership.

Not that there weren't rivals, always. It was part of the job, Chion knew. Rising to the challenge of assisting them into unthreatening roles of great acclaim was something she prided herself on. Without enemies, she had to admit to herself as she sat there scanning and stamping documents, the work would be in danger of getting boring.

Most of what she was approving that morning didn't bear reading beyond the memo title. Paychecks, work orders, supply allocations, punishment schedules, guard movements, all the things that kept Portlandtown running smoothly and peacefully. She had never tried to read the papers—honestly, it was too grim. It sapped her energy to dwell on all the signs of controlled failure, the sum of parts that didn't quite add up to a whole, functioning society. Even as a child she'd never had any illusions about the devastation she would step up to lead Cascadia out of. A plague that killed half the world's population, followed, at least in Cascadia, by decades of civil wars and famines that decimated the rest and broke down every system built and maintained by the valiant women of the first Formation.

Chion had always kept the long game in mind, and her belief in the redemptive vision of the Reformation had never wavered. A world of great industry and great progress was just over the horizon, she knew. The anarchists would come around to see it, too, once their last bicycle spoke broke and could not be replaced.

So she didn't read the papers, just took pleasure in the clockwork movement of her stamping. But the words on one document caught her eye just as her hand was coming down; she pulled her hand back, leaving only a red smudge from the edge of the stamp block. *Special Dispensation to Recruit New Guardian Corps Members from Low-Performing High Schools*. "In order to fill a shortage resulting from increased losses on guard duty," it read. Chion frowned. Guard attrition was far too high lately, and not all were apparent casualties—guards were either being killed, kidnapped, or defecting at the highest rate she'd seen. No threat of punishment seemed to slow the defection rate.

The collapse of the Reformation governments in Eugenetown and Salemtown had resulted in massive unrest and a major population shift. The anarchists were swelling in numbers and had increased their raids on Portlandtown's thriving factories, and more Guards than ever were needed to fend them off...and more were disappearing. If they could just hold them off a little longer... LaShonda's last report had reassured her that this overpopulation was only speeding along the onset of technological starvation that would lay the groundwork for lasting peace. It couldn't come soon enough for Chion.

Hell, someone needed to keep the perimeter peaceful. She was about to stamp the document when she saw who had already approved the requisition—her old school rival, Emily Hillhammer.

Now, that was concerning. Of course, someone from Education had to sign off on this, but Chion could see for the first time a way for Emily to snake her tendrils across silos and into the political realm—via military affairs, of all places. The woman was savvy. Savvier than she had given her credit for.

She set that page aside and continued stamping. Emily, she felt with quiet inner alertness, could be a worthy opponent after all. The path was faint this time, but inwardly she knew beyond a shadow of a doubt that here was the beginning of the first true challenge of her career. She saw clearly the necessity of military defense, but she could also just as clearly see the weak position occupied by her colleagues who had fallen into hating and fearing the anarchists. Chion had always been one to take a more measured stance, advocating a more humane defense— already the first segments were being fabricated of the great fence that would be her first legacy. The founders had said that outer peace would ultimately be a reflection of inner peace, and Chion's strength was always taking the essence of the founders' words to heart.

But inner peace was one of their more challenging teachings. And was it right to feel serene in the face of injustice? A great sense of indignation rose within her, and she pushed aside her half-completed pile of paperwork and returned to Emily's abominable order. She would look into the matter of these missing women thoroughly. And she would investigate this grave attempt to exploit young people for political ends.

Leaders did not usually require the rough disciplinary measures to correct their actions that ordinary people did. But Chion would not, she decided, rule out making an example of Emily Hillhammer for this travesty.

•   •   •

Kevin reached over and slapped the button to silence her alarm clock's clanging. She stretched her arms and legs and picked up the alarm clock to wind it, checking the time against the new light outside. The days were starting to get longer. Tonight, she would set the alarm a few minutes earlier. Give herself a bit more time. She pushed aside the covers. Her feet slapped against the warmth of the old wood floor and then the cool patio stones on the way to the outhouse. Back inside, she poured dried and pressed grain into a bowl, opened the hot water tap in her kitchen and kept her hand under the stream until it had reached its lukewarm peak temperature, then filled the bowl and covered it. The cooler the water, the longer it took to make the cereal edible. Today, she thought with a sigh, she'd be wolfing her food down on her way out the door, if she was lucky.

She went back into her bedroom, took the scrubs from the back of the chair, shook them out, and put them back on, then wrapped the thin blanket from the bed around her shoulders. Knowing it was futile, she went back into the kitchen to check the porridge. She swept the floor, wiped down the countertops, and went looking for more uses for the rag in her hand. Baseboards, those needed a swipe. Windowsills, too. She went back into her bedroom, made quick work of the surfaces there, and threw open the patio door. Just one step through, she froze. There was a rush of movement; it took a moment for her brain to process the reality of the girl who had jumped into the hedge next to the outhouse.

"Hello," said Kevin, not really sure what else to say. "What are you doing in the hedge?"

There was a rustle, then another, and then the girl crawled out. She was as small as all young people these days, making it hard to guess her age. She had olive skin and dark red hair, a distinctive genetic mix that Kevin admired professionally even amidst her confusion. The girl stood straight, with a determined grimace. She put a finger to her lips. "Please don't turn me in," she whispered.

Kevin made an instant decision and gestured to her door, waving the girl in ahead of her and shutting and locking it behind her. She then ushered the girl into the kitchen and poured half of her porridge into a second bowl. It was about as well soaked as it was going to be. She set the bowls on the table with her little jar of rice syrup in between, and waited.

The girl made no move toward her porridge bowl, appearing to be gathering her thoughts. "Thank you," she said finally.

"You're welcome," Kevin said. "I've been in a few difficult situations myself, in the past."

"My name's Lizi," said the girl, pushing out her story in one long breath. "My whole class is being recruited into the Guard today, so I split. My best friend went last year, and she's one of the ones who disappeared. I couldn't—I just—I'm no coward." She sat up straight. "But something is very wrong and I intend to find out what."

Kevin took a deep breath and released it.

"I'm not going to ask to stay here," Lizi said. "I'm on my way to my mother Emily's house. She always knows what to do."

Kevin shook her head. "Here might be a wiser choice," she pointed out. "When they look for you, they'll check with family first."

The girl's expression showed that she'd thought of that. "But you're a stranger. You'd risk being whipped in the square?"

"I've been before and survived," Kevin said. "My name is Kevin."

To her credit, Lizi showed only the briefest expression of surprise. "You're a mannist?"

"My mother was. She named me after her grandfather. She thought that men were the best lost hope for humanity. I grew up with the candles and chanting, the suicide pacts, the whole bit. I stopped believing in it when I was nine. It's no religion for little kids, that's for sure."

"But you were still beaten."

"Yes, I was thirteen when the Leaders decided to make an example of us. It's hard to prove your independence when you're that age."

"I know it!" Lizi said with an exaggerated sigh. Then, after a pause, "I'm sorry they hurt you."

Kevin shook her head. "It's how I learned to trust my own observations and be skeptical of other people's talk. That's served me well in my career." She jumped to her feet, downing the last of her porridge, which was now both tough and congealed. "Speaking of which, I'm about to be late. You'll stay here, then? There's a bit of food and plenty of books. I'll be home by dark."

"Thank you," Lizi said again.

"Of course."

Kevin walked out her front door into the hallway, pressed the heels of her hands to her eyes, took a deep breath, and set out for work.

Her route didn't normally take her past the old City Hall, but she could see a crowd spilling out onto the street from four blocks away and turned left instead of continuing straight toward the clinic.

"Bring back our girls!" the howl went up as she approached.

She felt her breath catch in the back of her throat as she saw the back of Chion Cyr's head. The Leader was walking away from the balcony, apparently before giving her promised speech.

"What's going on?" Kevin asked a woman who was hanging back from the crowd, watching.

"It got out that they're recruiting teenagers for Guard duty, taking them out of high school and sending them straight outside," the woman said. "And they're all disappearing already, you know? So the moms are pretty worked up about it. Cyr just tried to shift the blame and they're not having it."

"I wonder what's out there these days, on the outside," Kevin said, "and if it's really any worse than what's in here."

The woman raised an eyebrow, crossed her arms, and took half a step back, and Kevin beat a hasty retreat. What had gotten into her? She was very late for work now.

This morning she was testing zygote viability, a meditative process of grabbing a tube, tipping a drop of reagent into it, counting to ten, and setting it aside for washing and refilling—unless it turned blue. Only one in a thousand turned blue, which stressed out most of the other techs so the task tended to fall to Kevin. She found it restful, and it gave her thoughts structure and room to breathe. Which she needed today.

Whenever there was some new rule or edict from the Reform Council, Kevin always heard her mom's voice weighing in. She couldn't remember what her mother looked like, but her voice was distinct as ever, sometimes a pain in her ass and other times a real comfort to her. "We can always run away to join the anarchists" was one thing she would say, and this phrase had taken on a rich life in Kevin's imagination during the hardest times of her childhood. She had pictured the anarchists gathering herbs in the woods, herding goats, and occasionally breaking out of these mundane activities to brutally fight to the death over a perceived insult, with nobody around to punish or keep the peace. But was this real? The only fights Kevin had actually witnessed were the ones in her own school, between classes, in front of teachers too afraid to intervene. Early in the Reformation, she'd seen a woman knifed down in the street by Guards, and the whispers of "Mannist" had gone around. She'd run home terrified, knowing but not knowing the threat to her own home.

What was the threat, though? What had it ever been? Men weren't coming back. They were mythical creatures now, or might as well be, like unicorns or the Dodo bird. If you wanted to live your life regretting or celebrating their extinction, that showed more about how you felt about the living people around you than anything. Kevin's mom had believed that the plague that killed half the Earth's human population had been intentional, and she had spent her days gathering evidence against the "genocidal apologists" in the Reformation government while suspecting everyone around her of malicious minor deeds. Kevin thought the historical case might have some merit, but why care? Even if the pre-Reformation Leaders of the last century had killed off all the men on purpose, what did that matter now? It was done and gone.

I can always run off and join the anarchists, she thought again now. The test tube in her hand turned blue, and she set it in the empty tray to her left, but askew and with too much force, so that the seed of a future human splashed onto her scrubs. Well, shit. She stripped off her gloves and put her face in her hands. She thought of the bold, intelligent runaway in her apartment, risking everything so she could have a chance at surviving to an adulthood, and for what? To be killed by the anarchists Kevin was romanticizing, no doubt. But was it really a choice between life and death? It was a false choice, Kevin thought, not for the first time. What did Chion and the other Leaders offer, after all? A chance to defend a way of life marked by hunger, stifling rules, and brutal punishments? She knew that the anarchists had no mercy or social mores, but she also was old enough to remember the days of diplomacy and trading—food had been scarce and there were frequent outbreaks of fighting, but it hadn't been this... unrelenting.

Her thoughts were interrupted by the sound of a throat being cleared. Dara, the lab head, was standing at her elbow. Kevin jumped. "Good grief, Dara! How long have you been there?"

Dara, usually good humored, was not smiling. "Word just came from Reform Headquarters. They're cutting adult rations again."

"Well, shit." Kevin sighed. "Can you push back at all? We need steady hands for this."

Dara shook her head, lips a tight line. "They're cutting back on pregnancies, too. Too risky, too many mouths to feed." She held up a hand to prevent Kevin from speaking. "It's just temporary. But orders are orders. We're cutting back to baseline staff, enough to keep the current batch going but that's all. That means you can clock out early for the day."

"And come back when?" Kevin asked grimly.

"I wish I knew. I'll be right behind you as soon as I do the dishes and turn out the lights."

"Damn. Well come on over once you do, and I'll make you some tea while my hot water is still running." Dara was from the Evergreen Republic, she recalled, and would know exactly how to help Lizi escape north, if that's what the girl wanted to do. Maybe I should go too, Kevin thought. Staying seemed suddenly untenable.

"I'll do that," Dara said. "But between you and me, I won't stay long. If I'm going to make it past the patrols, I'll need to pack up and get moving right at dark."

"Going north?"

Dara raised an eyebrow. "East, actually. I've got some friends who live on a little farm out there. A little farm with a better army than ours. And," she winked, "no Leaders."

"Want to take someone with you?"

"You're looking to get out?"

"I'm tempted," Kevin said, "but I have a friend who needs it more. It'd be hard on you if you're caught with her, though."

"Harder than if I'm caught on my own? I'll bring your friend. And you too, if you change your mind by sunset."

Kevin dreaded waking up the next day in her apartment with nowhere to go and no way to replenish dwindling rations. But leaving, she saw in a flash, wasn't the right thing to do. Not just yet. She made another split second decision. "Go on to my place, you'll find my friend there unless she's taken another course of action. I'll try to come see you off, but I've got to go see an old friend first."

●　　●　　●

For the first time in her life, Chion did not know what to do. She saw no path forward. So she sat silently in her office in the waning day, staring out over the park across the street from Reformation Headquarters, her thoughts unformed and aimless. This mental wilderness was new to her, and terrifying. Joa, the head of the Guard, had told her that it wasn't safe for her to go into the streets while it was still daylight, and none of her work made sense in light of today's events, so she was just waiting, waiting until dark, waiting until she could see a way ahead again.

How had Emily done it? How long had she planned it? As early as their school days together? How many pieces of paper had she stamped that contained the early warning signs? Her coup was so subtle yet so total that Chion could hardly see the mechanism of it, much less any counter move.

So she sat. The answers would come, and her time would come. It always had.

What would you do, mother? she asked silently. Her mother came from a long, wealthy lineage of women who were powerful before most women had any power. But in her mind's eye, she saw only disappointment on her mother's face. Failure had never been an option for the Cyr clan.

There was a rap on the door frame, and Joa stepped in, standing as straight and strong as ever. "A citizen to see you," she said. "I said you weren't available, but it seems you know each other from school days."

Chion nodded. "Send her in."

At first she didn't recognize the woman, then suddenly she did, and a flood of warmth washed over her.

"Kevin."

"Chion. It's ... do you mind?"

"There's nobody I'd rather see," Chion said, remembering vividly the last time they'd parted ways, nearly two decades before. "I mean that. I'm sorry..."

"Me too. We were babies."

Chion grinned and shook her head. "No, I'm the one who owes you an apology. I thought you'd hurt my career. Because of your family. It was a decision of pure logic, and it hurt both of us. And... I was wrong. Today I lost everything..."

Kevin shook her head. "You mean this morning? I was in the crowd, it was on my way to work. That's why I'm here. Look, I understand what you've been trying to do here, but you do realize it's not working, right?"

"It can work. It would have. I just needed a little more time."

"I don't know about that," said Kevin. "Do you realize what's happening here? It's not just political. We don't have anything to eat. You can't push people any further without giving us something to make it worthwhile."

"It's not me you need to make this speech to. Emily Hillhammer, she'll be the Leader before the week is out. You can probably catch her over at the Education offices if you walk quickly."

"Look," Kevin said, "I'm just here to offer you a way out. There's a farm you can go to, with people who won't know who you are. You can get yourself some healthy food, get some perspective."

"This is my city, my whole world."

"Well, I don't know if it'll be any better there, and you don't have to stay there forever. But you can't stay here right now."

•　　　•　　　•

None of the younger ones could believe it, especially after she schooled them in the practice yard, but Mayana was old enough to remember men. They loomed darkly in all of her earliest memories, mostly sick, dying, and being mourned during the plague years. They had once run the world, her mother had told her, but their strength and vitality had withered in retribution for misusing their power.

Maybe it was time for a new plague, she thought. She was sitting cross-legged on the foundation of the new dormitory they were building on the grounds of what had long ago been a resort for the wealthy, and before that a farm for the poor. Now it had come full circle. She was looking over the practice yard where Ko was training the new recruits in basic hand-to-hand combat skills. The recruits were diverse in age and skin tone, but united by the basic factors of hunger, anger, and the expectation of punishment. It caused most of them to hold back from the fight, except for the few who went recklessly ballistic. Ko was noticing the same tendencies and deftly sorting them into new pairings by skill and temperament. Her transformation amazed Mayana most of all.

Mayana remembered more than just the reality of men. She remembered what it had meant to be a woman. Dresses, dolls, a certain way of being spoken to and being expected to speak... She could barely recall the details, just that every ounce of her young soul had rebelled, had driven her hard in the opposite direction: to fighting, to dirty work, to strength for its own sake, to decisive action and judgment, to keeping herself apart. When her mother had taken the two of them to live with the militia, the adolescent Mayana had never been happier. It had suited her to live most of her life at war. She watched as Ko exchanged a soft look with one of the recruits and let her hand linger on the red-headed young woman's shoulder as she corrected her stance, before facing off and expediently throwing the other woman smoothly over her shoulder, knocking the breath out of her.

Mayana envied these young people nothing, but she felt a pang for their freedom from that inner partition. There were no more women in the world, she thought, any more than there were any men. Not by the old meanings of the word. And with the next generation there would be, she hoped, no more Mannism, and only the fading light of the Reformation's womanist ideology. With every egg fertilized by hand in a clinic, selected solely for viability, the old concept of inherited race had been turned inside out—ha, there was a concept that was almost impossible to explain to the kids. *Even so,* she thought, *we've managed to invent new lines to divide ourselves.*

An older woman, who Mayana recognized by her quaint masculine name, Kevin, had stepped to the sidelines, breathing hard and holding her side. Mayana unfolded herself from her perch and went over to her.

"I'm not sure I'm cut out for anarchism after all," said Kevin.

Mayana laughed. "Not everyone needs to send the Reformation flying on its ass. But it's good to know the basics. They'll be sending a force after us soon enough."

"A force of hungry, untrained children," Kevin said. "You could defeat them with a pot of soup."

"Can you cook, then? We could always use a stronger defense in that area."

"I love to. Possibly more to the point, I've spent my career creating and raising viable zygotes," Kevin said. "Do you make babies out here?"

"Not yet." Mayana gestured to the two dozen new recruits. "Listen, tough it out another week through defense training, and then someone, probably LaShonda, will sit down with you and get your full skill profile. You'll likely end up cooking because we always need folks who can do that. The younger recruits grew up without a lot of food so none of them know how to make it taste good." She made a face and Kevin grinned.

"But our record keeping is no good, so keep bringing it up that you can make babies, ok? They're not much good in a fight, but we'll need them someday, I hope."

"Can I ask how long you've been out here?" Kevin said. "I know you have no leaders, but you look—well, if I didn't know better I'd say you were in charge."

"I've been here the whole time," Mayana said.

"Would you be authorized to negotiate, say, a treaty?"

Mayana barked a laugh of surprise. "A treaty? Who is negotiating treaties?"

"Well," Kevin said, "it's complicated."

•   •   •

Ko breathed in, out, pedaled, coasted, slowed, pedaled again. Ahead of her, the great Leader of the Reformation rode on the front rack of another former Guard's bike, head held high, looking for everything in the world like she was leading an army into battle, like it was her own idea.

Ko hadn't been involved in the negotiations, but Lizi had told her about it later. Chion hadn't wanted to accept that these quiet farmers were the same lawless anarchists she'd spent her career seeking to conquer and destroy, but she had adjusted with great agility to the idea that she could take a leadership role in overturning the corrupt bureaucrats who had ousted her from Reform Headquarters.

"LaShonda played it brilliantly," Lizi had confided to Ko afterward, as they sat close together reinforcing leather armor straps at the edge of the circle of firelight in the central clearing. "They went to school together, along with mother Emily, so she knew just how to finesse it. So now it's officially Cyr's great charge to retake her homeland and establish peaceful trade with us, and probably with Evergreen too. She's already coming up with slogans. 'Now We Reform the Reformation' and 'The Human Condition of Peace and Prosperity.' Can you even believe her?"

Lizi had laughed heartily at her own telling of the story, and only stopped when she saw the tears on Ko's face. "I'm sorry, love, you lost your friends to all this foolishness. It must not be funny to you at all. Can you forgive me?"

Ko could and did forgive Lizi anything, far more quickly and easily than she'd forgiven the anarchists, or had forgiven herself for her defection and the violence she'd brought against her own former cohort since. She was still amazed at how quickly a little food, acceptance, and a sense of belonging could override a lifetime of ingrained loyalties and fears. But now, riding in formation behind Chion Cyr, forgiveness was out of reach. She found she was highly aware of the staff strapped across her own back, how little it would take to release the straps, the way it would feel in her hand as she swung it around, the shock to her joints as it connected with the spot right behind the Leader's ear.

Not doing it took every ounce of the courage and discipline that she'd developed in the year since coming to live at Edgefield. She kept her hands at her sides and kept walking. She thought about the younger sisters in her old family compound. *They need to eat. They need a chance at a future worth looking forward to.*

Ko would stay in Portlandtown for a while to make sure of it. Make sure her sisters got food, make sure that things at Reformation Headquarters didn't go back to business as usual. Staff at the ready, always a step away.

Ahead of her, she heard a rustling, saw a gleam of metal, recognized it as the buckle of leather armor. Ko whooped a warning and leapt off her bicycle in a graceful move, seeing it roll into the bushes on the side of the track in her perpheral vision. She snapped her staff into position an instant before the first guard came at her with her blade drawn.

In the long moment before their weapons met, Ko felt the anger rushing cleanly through her. She would survive this and fight again, she knew. There would always be another battle. All the cooperative, peaceful ideology of womanism or the quiet, monkish agrarianism of the anarchists couldn't prevent this war, or stop her from having to kill a petrified teenager who could have been her sister and was now inexpertly thrusting a long knife at her.

She calibrated the single blow of her staff to knock unconscious rather than kill. She wasn't sure she'd gotten it quite right, but there was no time to check—she rushed off to help protect Cyr.

This is courage, this is freedom, she thought furiously, taking out another Guard from behind with a swipe of her staff, swiveling around and looking for more. *To choose a path forward and follow it boldly as far as you can, even when you know it's just as horrific a choice as all the others.*

The young forest was quiet now, the only sounds her companions' ragged breathing. This path, she knew, led her back to Portlandtown, but what would it mean when she got there? Was it home or the enemy or both? Or neither?

Ko sighed, shunted her staff into the straps on her back, and went back to look for the young soldier she'd knocked flat. If she had survived, Ko promised herself, she would teach her, if she was willing, to fight and cook and choose boldly between all the terrible options the world offered.

FAST LEARNER

Kris Rose

I don't know why I thought this show would be any different than the rest. I had actually convinced myself for a moment that tonight I would have a good time, would talk to new and interesting people, and wouldn't feel intimidated or left out by the teenage groupies that followed Raymond around like lost puppies. It was the same story every single weekend of the few months we'd lived in this town, yet I never learned my lesson.

As I surveyed the warehouse, I was pretty sure this would be the same old thing as always. At the ripe old age of 25, I felt jaded amongst all these obnoxious 21 year olds with their enthusiasm and their dance moves. The girls were competitive and much too fashionable. The guys were uptight and humorless, even more fashion-conscious than some of the girls.

I was drinking a beer and had several more stashed in my shoulder bag just in case. I couldn't face this crowd sober, but I had sworn off of painkillers after my last habit had landed me in rehab over a year earlier. I hadn't been 100% clean since, but a few Vicodin here and there when I was in actual pain didn't seem to me to be cheating—not if I really needed it and as long as I stopped once the pain stopped.

These were rules my non-drug addict husband didn't understand or agree with, so I just didn't tell him about it. Raymond and I had met just a few months after I had quit heroin and he was always so ready to bust me for relapsing that sometimes it was almost as if he wanted me to relapse. I was almost certain there were things he wasn't telling me, either.

Raymond was bringing in equipment and making the rounds, so I had already ceased to exist as far as he was concerned. Nobody else at the show seemed to give much of a shit that I was there either; familiar strangers with a few of Raymond's friends thrown in. A few of them seemed cool, but I was still an outsider.

The show consisted of a few bands in a dirty warehouse, my husband's band included, along with some brutally disgusting homebrew that a dreadlocked hippie was trying to pass off as real alcohol. I wasn't excited about poisoning myself with whatever heinous concoction he had created, but I knew once the beer I had brought with me ran out, I wouldn't much care what I was drinking—as long as it kept the steady buzz of oblivion coursing through my body.

I decided to find Raymond and ride his social coattails for a while. When I caught up to him, he was with a small group of people, including his old friend Gil, who I had met on several occasions and who had always gone out of his way to include me.

"Hey Missy! How are you?" Gil asked me.

"I'm fine," I lied, smiling politely and effectively killing the conversation with my awkwardness once again.

I stood next to Raymond, waiting for him to acknowledge me in any way, but he was in the middle of trash talking someone I barely knew, which was par for the course with Ray.

"He didn't even know who Hickey was before I gave him a mixed tape a year ago with some songs on it. Now he acts like he's known about them forever; it's pathetic. He never even went to a live show. He's just like all the other poseurs around here."

Everyone stood around not saying anything and nodding their heads.

"I thought he was sweet, actually," I finally said. Ray's nostrils twitched in agitation.

"Yeah, he's a nice kid," Gil chimed in, and Ray's nostrils twitched double time.

After a few minutes of other random chit-chat, people wandered off and Ray and I were left alone at last. I could tell he was still fuming from my earlier comment.

"So . . ." I began, but Ray cut me off, leaning down close to my face so nobody else could hear him.

"The only reason you think that asshole is so nice is because you want to fuck him!"

"Jesus, Ray, I do not, I just don't think it's such a crime to learn about bands later than other people, that's all! You're so harsh on everyone all the time; nobody meets your standards! Not even me! *Especially* not me!" My voice started to get loud and Ray looked around nervously.

"Maybe I wouldn't lose my patience with you so much if you'd go out and start making your own friends and get a life of your own instead of relying on me for everything!"

"Fuck you!" I was already on the verge of tears and it wasn't even 10 p.m. "You never let me out of your *sight* when we lived in Arkansas! I couldn't even go out to the bar with my girlfriends for one night without you showing up and making a scene, accusing me of trying to meet up with other men. I left everything and everyone to follow you here because you said you wanted me here. Now you act like I'm smothering you. Make up your mind so I can get on with my life."

Raymond looked off into the distance. "I didn't force you to do anything. I never have. You made your own choices. It's not my problem. You are not my problem."

He walked off, towards his most recent bass player, Hannah. I watched his entire demeanor change as he approached her. His shoulders relaxed, his face lit up—he was a completely different person than ten seconds ago. If you met him like this, you would never expect him to be so cruel. I certainly hadn't. I had fallen for his act completely. I was still falling for it, apparently. As I stood there, I began to realize that guys like Ray would always get away with being dicks, but only because of girls like me.

That was the thought going through my head when I heard the first screams.

It was hard in the chaos to figure out exactly what was going on, but I could tell that some people were gathered around something in the other room. As I pushed my way through the crowd, I saw a guy crumpled on the floor, convulsing, blood coming from everywhere—his eyes, ears, mouth, even his pants were quickly becoming soaked in blood in the front and back.

People were crying and hiding their faces, yet doing nothing to help the guy. Eventually a boy with dreads pulled out his phone to call 911. A few seconds later, he announced that the emergency number was busy. Nobody was coming to help this guy who was seemingly dying right in front of us.

As if on cue, seven or eight more people dropped to the floor and began convulsing. This caused a surge of people to run for the exits. I'm not sure why I wasn't one of them, except that I had no idea where Raymond was and it didn't seem like a good idea to leave without him. He was my husband and I loved him, sure. I also had no idea where we were in the city or how to get back to our house.

I tried calling Raymond's phone and got a message saying, "All circuits are busy at this time." I kept searching around the warehouse, going room to room, looking everywhere and asking if anyone had seen him, but people were too involved in the process of freaking out.

I finally spotted Raymond coming out of the bathroom. I waved frantically with relief, but he didn't see me as he quickly slunk around the corner and into the other room. I began to run after him when the door opened again and out stepped his bass player Hannah.

I stopped dead in my tracks and watched her slink off in the opposite direction. For the first time that night I felt a wave of cold panic crash over me. My whole world fell apart just minutes after the actual world fell apart. My arms started to have that familiar tingle that they get when I'm about to have a panic attack. My vision started to get cloudy and things started to look dimmer, kind of flattened out. Just as I was on the verge of losing it altogether, I felt somebody crash into me and was knocked to the floor.

The girl who had knocked me over was lying next to me, blood seeping out from her eye sockets, eyes rolled back into her head so that only the whites were showing. I lay there in shock and watched her, unable to do anything until I felt somebody pulling me up by my arms. It was Raymond's friend Gil.

"Are you okay?" he asked with real concern. "I saw you go down from across the room—are you hurt?"

I shook my head. I was not physically harmed.

"Let's get you upstairs. The owner of the warehouse has an apartment up there. A few of us are hiding out there until the cops or somebody comes."

I followed him up the stairs and stood behind him as he did a little knock: Shave and a haircut, two bits. "It's Gil!" he shouted over the noise of downstairs.

The door opened a crack and the dreadlocked hippie poked his head out long enough to see who it was, "C'mon in man, hurry up!"

"I've got Missy with me, Raymond's wife."

"Cool, cool, get in here."

I stepped into the room and saw Raymond sitting on the floor next to some other random people and our friend Evie. The bastard hadn't even bothered to try and find me before saving his own skin. I looked around but didn't see Hannah at first. I thought gleefully that perhaps she was bleeding out her eyeballs downstairs by now, but then immediately felt awful. Just then I saw her in the apartment's kitchen and all guilt vanished, replaced by bloodlust once again. Raymond met my eyes and waved at me to come sit next to him. Evie scooted over just enough to make a space for me. I hated myself for going over there, but where else would I go? I tried to tell myself that I only suspected, I didn't know, but that was bullshit. I totally knew. Everybody knew.

"Okay guys! Listen up!" a tall, older man with a large beard came into the center of the large room. About twenty-five of us sat in a circle facing him.

"My name is Stan . . ."

I felt Raymond's tangled mop of hair brush against my cheek as he leaned over to whisper in my ear, "That Stan guy? I heard he slept with a bunch of fifteen year olds and went to prison for a few years."

I turned to face him, saying nothing. I was shocked that even with all this going on around him, he could still be so concerned with knocking some guy down a few pegs for my benefit, and right after he had been fooling around with some other girl. Was he really this sick? I was on the verge of falling apart and I barely knew these people dying around me, but these were his friends he had grown up with. People he'd known his entire life dropping dead in front of his eyes and his priorities are getting some on the side and making sure I'm not attracted to the guy who might save our lives. "Are you serious right now?" I whispered. I could see that the anger and disbelief on my face surprised him.

What the fuck was this Stan guy saying anyway? I could literally die because I was too busy dealing with Raymond's stupid drama. That would be just about perfect.

". . . so we think that the people who are sick down there are the ones who *didn't* drink any of Matt's homebrewed wine. Can we real quick have a show of hands up here for everyone who *has* had some of the wine tonight?"

I raised my hand, as did everyone else in the room, but to be honest I wasn't sure if I should. I had tasted only a sip of the vile stuff and had been waiting until I ran out of my own beer before trying to attempt drinking any more. Could a sip really be enough to make me immune? And why the hell would his homebrew be any better than what you get from the store? It sounded like hippie bullshit to me, but it was keeping the crowd calm for now, and that had to be good. The last thing we wanted was more panic. More than we already had, anyway.

"Okay, good, that's good. We've got several gallons of the stuff stashed up here for the time being. If it is some sort of antidote, then we need to find out if one drink is enough to keep you safe or if we have to keep drinking it at a certain rate. We need a control, basically a volunteer who will agree to stop drinking now while the rest of us keep drinking so we can see if they get sick."

Everyone in the room suddenly got very, very quiet, looking at their cups of wine, or the floor, or their shoes, anywhere but up. I was in the middle of debating whether or not to raise my hand when I heard Stan make the announcement.

"Okay people, it looks like we have a volunteer," Stan called out. "Let's hear it for Gil!" I snatched my head up to see Gil make his way towards the center of the room where Stan handed him a bottle of water. Everyone clapped gratefully and relieved smiles and laughs rippled through the crowd. "Go Gil!" "Right on man!" "You're awesome!"

I felt pretty confident that Gil wouldn't be putting himself in any real danger. In fact, he might be at an advantage over everyone still drinking that crap. It couldn't be the shitty beer, but what could it be? What did everyone still keeping their blood on the inside of their eyes have in common?

That's when Matt began foaming bloody saliva at the mouth and people really lost their shit. Without the "beer cure," there was nothing holding people's hopes together and most people just started crying. Stan and Gil moved brewmaster Matt into his bed in the other room under the guise of making him more comfortable, but really to make the rest of us more comfortable.

It was getting close to 1 a.m. and most of us were beyond drunk. I was beginning to get kind of loopy, my thoughts jumping around between possibly confronting Raymond and trying to remember everything I had learned in the science classes at community college. I was still drunk, but not shit-faced. In fact, the thing I felt most right then was tired, not to mention snippy towards Raymond and disgusted with that traitor Hannah. So much for feminism, bitch.

I went to the bedroom. Gil was sitting beside Matt, who I could see from the doorway was no longer convulsing or moving around in any way.

"Is he . . . ?" I asked quietly.

Gil looked up and nodded his head, "Yeah, just a few minutes ago."

"I'm sorry. Was he a close friend?"

"Not really, but he was still a good guy. He didn't deserve to die like this."

"Does anyone?" I asked, secretly thinking that yes, maybe a few bass players deserved this kind of death. No, I realized— feeling ashamed of myself for placing more blame on the girl than the guy—both of them deserve this death.

"Believe it or not, I'm starting to get really tired," I said instead. I sat down on the floor.

"I have something for that, actually." Gil reached into his bag and pulled out a small prescription pill bottle. "Adderall." He smiled and tossed it towards me and I caught it in both hands.

I shook the nearly full bottle. "Mating call of my home state." I smiled and Gil smiled back.

"Where's that?" he asked.

"Arkansas, home of the Razorbacks. How many?" I asked, unscrewing the cap.

"Start with two and see how you feel after half an hour."

I took out two pills and Gil handed me a bottle of water to wash them down. I started to hand the pill bottle back to him but he shook his head. "Keep them."

I shrugged and put them into my front pocket, grateful that the people in this town were so generous with their drugs, unlike back home.

"What's going on? What are we going to do?" I asked Gil, but also nobody in particular.

"I'm sorry about Raymond and Hannah," he said suddenly.

I looked at him without saying anything.

"I should have said something, I wanted to . . . but . . . we've been friends such a long time and I didn't even know if you'd believe me or not. I didn't want to blow up your marriage over a suspicion."

"I saw them come out of the bathroom together tonight," I said.

"Shit," Gil replied with sympathy.

"Yeah well, who's the bigger asshole? He's the one with a wife, but it's still disappointing. I guess I knew she and I weren't close, but I thought of her as a sort of friend. Why girls choose to fuck each other over for asshole guys I'll never know."

"What are you gonna do?"

"I have no idea," I answered honestly.

I stared out into space. I guess I had always suspected something was up. I had begged Ray not to have Hannah join the band, arguing the point that she didn't even know how to play the bass. He had laughed at me and said I was being irrational. I had asked if I could learn to play the bass and be in the band instead. All he'd said was, "Hannah's a fast learner."

Gil broke the silence.

"Jesus, look, let's get out of here and find something to eat. You starting to feel those pills yet?"

I noticed a nice steady thrumming in my veins, like electricity coursing through all my muscles at once, everything connected. "Yeah, I think so."

"Okay, well let's put some food into you before you don't want it anymore."

As I stood up I saw something poking out from a shelf above the bed. It was a metal box, military green. I reached up and took it down, unlatching and opening it before I could really think about the fact that I was snooping around in a dead man's room while he was still in it. Inside was an old Colt automatic handgun.

"Wow!" Gil said, looking over my shoulder. "That's a gun."

I met his eyes as I picked it up out of the case. He didn't seem alarmed at all, which I found refreshing in this city with its anti-gun, pro-veganism mentality. I took off the safety and pulled back the slide, making sure the barrel was pointing at the floor. There was no round in the chamber, but when I slid out the magazine, it was filled to the top.

"You really know what you're doing with that thing!" Gil said, obviously impressed.

"Yeah, my grandfather taught me how to handle a gun when I was seven years old. It's like riding a bike."

Gil's face went serious.

"Speaking of bikes, I know it sounds terrible, but I have an idea about what we should do next. Do you want to hear it?"

I nodded yes and slipped the safety back into place, sliding the Colt into my bag. After all, Dreadlocks didn't need it any longer.

Gil's plan was simple. The roads would be clogged with people trying to escape by car, so we would ride our bikes about forty miles outside of the city to a nearby lake where Gil's family owned a small island. On the island sat a nice-sized house with plenty of supplies for all the remaining people plus any family members who managed to find their own way there before the plague got them.

"I don't have a bike, Gil. Raymond and I drove here."

"Well, here's where the plan gets a little messy."

After Gil and I left the bedroom and he announced Matt's death, and his version of a plan, a small group of us went back downstairs and dug through the pockets of the dead until we had found enough keys to unlock enough bikes for everyone still alive who didn't refuse to use a dead person's bike. In rare form, Raymond was right next to me the entire time, ironically acting beyond possessive and paranoid. Maybe *he* would have thought to have an illicit affair in the same room as a recently dead body, but revenge sex was honestly the last thing on my mind at the time. We reluctantly went through all the dead people's bags too, looking for patch kits, extra tubes, cans of fix-a-flat, anything that we might need while riding through the city and into the country.

"Gil, how the fuck am I going to ride a bike 40 miles?" I asked with real concern.

I hadn't been on a bike in years, even though I had been an avid cyclist in my early teens. I used to ride my bike out in the country with a cigarette dangling from the corner of my mouth, not even winded, let alone gasping for breath the way I did now whenever I even walked up a semi-steep incline.

"Don't worry. I'll help you out if you get into trouble. We're not leaving anyone behind."

I looked over at Raymond, who just happened to be avoiding Hannah who I could now see was staring daggers into his back as he packed up his messenger bag with supplies. Everyone else who planned on going was doing the same thing, about twenty-two in all. Strangely enough, the group was turning into mostly girls. In the time it took for us to pitch the plan, agree upon its execution, and start making the bikes and ourselves roadworthy, four more guys had dropped from our group, leaving eighteen of us, twelve of whom were girls that I had seen around or knew fairly well. We were all downstairs making good our escape while the abstainers waited it out in Matt's apartment upstairs—waiting for what, I didn't know.

It was clear some people were starting to get tired and sloppy from all the booze. Some people had apparently not realized that Matt's death had ended our science experiment and were filling empty water bottles with the homebrew—or maybe they were just trying to numb themselves to what promised to be a real horror show outside. The thought made me feel a little less angry towards my cheating husband. After all, either one of us could be dead in fifteen minutes' time.

"Raymond?" I went over to my husband as he started loading up his bike. "Here," I placed two of the little yellow pills into his hand. "Take these to help keep you awake on the ride."

"Fuck yes!" he immediately recognized the pills and grabbed his water and eagerly washed them down. Then he looked at me suspiciously. "Wait, why do you have these?"

"They're not mine, they're Gil's, for his ADD."

"Oh really?" he cocked his head, pursing his lips. "You and Gil have certainly been spending a lot of time together tonight."

I sighed and closed my eyes, not at all willing to play this game with him. Not now; not when we could all be dying at any moment.

"That's right Raymond, I've been hanging out with Gil, because unlike you, he gives a shit about how I'm doing during all of this." I gestured around me to the dead bodies still leaking blood all over the warehouse floor.

"Whatever," Raymond snorted out his nose, a nervous tic he gets when he knows he's under scrutiny. "You're a big girl, you can take care of yourself."

Just then, I noticed that Hannah was standing right next to us.

"Raymond, can you help me with my bike for a minute?" she asked. She glared at me, waiting for me to say or do something I guess, but I was starting to care less and less about her stupid drama and wonder more why I needed so much of my own. We stood in awkward silence while Raymond pointedly ignored her, pretending to adjust his chain. Hannah looked like she wanted to cry before finally huffing and puffing back to her own bike, which had the front wheel taken off, stupid little blue sparkly decorations on the spokes, and what looked like a tube poking out from underneath the tire.

"You should go help her," I said. He looked at me in surprise. "Really, go."

He started to walk away, hesitated, and then walked back quickly. I thought that he might confess his sins, but no.

"Can I get one more of those pills first?" I rolled my eyes and pulled the bottle out once more. "Maybe two more?" He made his eyes wide, trying his best to be charming. Unbelievable nerve.

"Fine." I took out two of the pills and handed them to him. He swallowed them dry, something I could never do, not even at the peak of my addiction.

In about an hour's time we had everyone collected who was still able to ride a bike. Gil and I passed out pills. Evie looked at me guiltily as I handed her pills and water.

"Don't worry Evie, this doesn't mean you're relapsing or anything, it's just to get us where we're going."

"I'm so sorry," she said with tears welling up in her eyes.

"What are you talking about? You're drunk. Stop talking silly and let's get you on your bike. You're just lucky you have your own. I'm riding some poor dead person's bike and besides that I haven't even touched one in almost ten years!" I smiled at her, trying to lighten her mood.

"I thought that you two were over, he told me that you weren't together anymore," she croaked as tears started to stream down her face.

"Oh fuck!" The pit in my stomach that I thought couldn't grow any larger swelled with the knowledge of what she was telling me. *Not her too! You son of a bitch!* I thought. Unlike Hannah, who was my acquaintance by force, Evie was a real friend, or at least I had thought so. I looked at her chubby face, wet with tears, her eyes full of real remorse, and I felt my anger toward her dissipate.

Evie wasn't the true enemy here. She had been duped just as I had been duped. A pattern I had allowed to continue because I was too afraid of being without him to confront him about his shitty behavior. I was afraid at first of being left behind in Arkansas while he moved on to bigger and better things, and then after we moved I was afraid of being left alone in a bigger city without any friends or support system. I knew exactly how alone and vulnerable Evie had felt over the past six months because we'd talked about it once over several bottles of cheap wine. I could see it clearly, how easy it must have been for Raymond to take advantage of that situation. Why Evie? Why Hannah? What I really wanted to ask Raymond was if he thought I had been an easy target, too. I was afraid the answer would have been "yes."

I gave Evie a tight hug.

"It's okay Evie, I'm not mad, really. Not at you." I let her go and handed her a water. "Now take those pills, okay?"

She nodded her head and sniffled like a little kid, taking a drink of water and then tossing both pills towards the back of her throat. I looked over to where Raymond was helping Hannah put her tube back on the wheel.

"Motherfucker!" I muttered angrily.

"Please don't tell him that I told you!" Evie said, obviously still worried what Raymond thought about her. That only made me angrier at him. Why should anyone give a fuck about what a liar and cheater like him thought? Why did *I*?

"I won't, don't worry. It doesn't matter anymore, anyway." I smiled tightly, a fake smile, and saw the concern in her eyes. She and I both knew I was lying.

***

The streets on the way to the bike trail were full of cars that were mostly abandoned or the drivers and passengers were dead. The smell of excrement made it harder to ignore the fact of what we were riding past and through. Mostly I just breathed through my mouth and let the pills do their numbing, tingly thing until we reached the sanctuary of the bike trail.

It wasn't until mile nine on the trail that we suffered our first casualty. He wasn't anyone that I knew well, just some guy that was always around at all the shows, but it still hit me hard to see him writhing on the asphalt next to his bike. I stepped off of my own bike and reached into my bag, grabbing the gun. When the others began to realize what it was and what I was about to do, I heard a few screams before the deafening sound of gunfire drowned them out.

The guy was still now. The ringing in my ears made the scene seem even more unreal. A head shot, no mistakes, no more suffering. My knees started to buckle as I felt somebody steady me from behind.

"It's okay," said the guy who'd grabbed me. It was Stan. "There wasn't anything else to be done. You did him a favor."

I looked around and saw that several people had ridden off, maybe thinking that I was going to shoot them all in a rampage of bullets. That would have been a waste of ammo. But, I thought smugly to myself, what do these people know about things like that?

I noticed that one of the missing bikes was Hannah's. Then I noticed that another was Raymond's. "That fucking coward," I muttered as I got back onto my bike, getting some sympathetic glances as well as wary ones. After about half a mile I announced that I was stopping to pee. I dropped my bike into the grass and headed towards some brush where I promptly threw up.

The remaining twelve of us kept going. Apparently while I was puking, Stan and Gil had assured everyone that I was not a bloodthirsty maniac hell-bent on killing them all. One girl decided not to take her chances and went off on her own at a break in the trail. I wasn't hurt by it, I could understand her point of view, especially if she had also somehow managed to fuck Raymond behind my back. What I was, however, was very, very tired. So out came the little yellow pills.

Soon, I was close to being the last person in line. Next to me was a small girl who looked to be around seventeen. When she saw me looking at her she timidly introduced herself as Sasha and said that she had met Raymond a few years ago when he had come through her town on tour with his old band.

"So what? You're going to tell me that you slept with him too?" I laughed, expecting her to laugh along with me, but when I looked over she was staring hard away and I knew, punched in the gut once again.

"But you're a baby!"

"I'm twenty-one," she said quietly. "I was eighteen at the time. We kept in touch through email for a while, but then he stopped. To be honest, I moved here still thinking we could make it work, but then I found out he was married . . ."

She looked at me seriously and then looked back to the ground.

"Well," I sighed, "at least you have some respect for that fact. The girls around here don't seem to give a shit one way or the other."

"I wasn't raised that way, to break up people's marriages," she said with feeling. "My dad left me and my mom for another woman. It destroyed my mom. I would never do that to anyone." I could hear her voice starting to crack.

"It's okay, Sasha, I believe you," I said gently.

We rode along together for a few miles. Sasha made small talk while I tried to remember all the reasons I had ever thought moving out here with Raymond was such a good idea. How had I allowed this to go so far? How much more was I willing to take from him before enough was enough? I was lost in this train of thought when I heard yelling from the front of the line.

By the time Sasha and I caught up to everyone else, it was clear that something big was going on.

It was Raymond, coming from God knows where, scared and out of breath and riding towards us on a girl's bike. The bike looked familiar—then it hit me. This was Hannah's bike. I recognized the blue sparkly beads on that stupid front tire she had needed so much help with.

We gathered around Raymond while he calmed down, waiting to hear what had him so upset. I was anxious to hear why the hell he had ridden off in the first place. He took a deep breath and began, "I saw Hannah and two other girls ride off when they saw the gun," he met my eyes only briefly then quickly looked away again. "I tried to go after them, but my bike got a flat and I started walking it towards where I thought they were going when I saw this big group of bikers surround them. There wasn't anything I could do, they just took them. They had guns and there were so many of them, I couldn't do a thing." He punctuated this last statement with a choked sob and put his face into his hands as a few girls rushed forward to comfort and reassure him.

As I watched Raymond telling his story, I saw how he widened his eyes whenever he started to go into detail—a sure sign that he was lying his ass off. He spotted me and read the look of doubt on my face instantly. He dropped Hannah's bike and ran over to hug me in front of the group.

"I didn't know if I'd ever see you again!" he cried into my neck, shaking his shoulders so that everyone could see how distraught he was.

I patted him on the back dispassionately. "It's okay, you're okay," I said, while thinking, *You motherfucker . . . what are you hiding?* to myself over and over again. For the first time, I was a little afraid of my own husband and what he might lie about.

The sun came up on mile 35 and we were at the Marina a few hours later. The weather was chilly—early summer here wasn't as warm as what I was used to back home. Limping towards the finish line, all of us looked crazy, and most of us were full of speed, coming down from speed, hungover, or still drunk. The Marina had a small bar that actually appeared to be open. I went inside with Gil and Stan to get the keys to Gil's parents' boat that they kept in a locker there. The bartender looked unconcerned that the world was ending and asked me if I wanted anything to drink.

"A beer, thanks." I sat on my stool and waited for the boys.

Stan came walking briskly towards me, his eyes wide with shock.

"You have to come with me, quickly. Is anyone else in here?"

"No! What the hell . . . ?"

"Shhh . . ." he put his finger up to his lips. "C'mon!" he shout-whispered.

Luckily, the bartender didn't give a fuck and handed me my beer without making any eye contact.

"Two dollars," he said to the wall.

I pulled out three dollar bills from my front pocket and took my beer into the back room following right behind Stan.

In the pool table room, near the bathrooms, stood one of the missing girls, Geena. She was playing pool by herself and obviously way, way drunk.

"She's not going to fucking shoot me, izz she?" she slurred, pointing the pool cue in my direction.

"No, I'm not going to shoot you . . . yet."

"What!?" she said alarmed. "What did she say?"

"Nothing, just tell Missy what you told me a few seconds ago," Stan said.

"Oh, your little husband, Raymond. Yeah, I used to fuck him back in the day, before he was married to you . . . I think," she snorted. "When you pulled out that gun, he told us that we were next because you had found out that he had fucked all of us, so we better get the fuck out of there before you killed us all."

"Wait . . ." I stopped her, "are you saying that he had had sex with *all three* of you girls at one point or another?"

She nodded in the affirmative while taking a sip from the straw sticking out of her giant mixed drink.

"He's fucked every single girl in town as far as I know," she declared before adding a weak, "Shorry."

"It's fine, really, just go on." I waved my hand at her to continue as I grabbed for my own drink. Things were finally beginning to come together in my mind.

"Well anyway, we didn't make it very far before we came up on all these biker guysh on motorcycles who stopped us and started harassing us for money. Raymond gave them his credit cards and then the next thing I know he's off in the dark talking with them alone, leaving ush to just sit and wait. Next thing you know, me and Hannah and that other girl are being dragged off by these guys and they're saying that they bought us from Raymond for a gram of meth."

Stan looked at me for a few moments before I realized he was waiting for my response.

"So why are you here? In this bar?" I asked.

"Oh yeah, turns out my uncle is a member of their club in Tarzana. So, they offered me a job selling meth out of the bar. It's not so bad. Free drinksh! Whoohoo!" She raised her glass, sloshing the drink onto her arm, which she immediately brought to her mouth to lick clean.

"That's great, but what about Hannah and the other girl?" I asked, reminding myself that I really shouldn't give a shit.

"Mmmm? I don't know . . . I guess they're still at the clubhoush."

"So . . ." I asked her, a plan already forming in my mind, ". . . you selling anything besides meth?"

***

When Gil came back with the keys to the family boat, Stan and I filled him in on the news. I let both of them know my theory on what exactly was going on with our miraculous plague immunity.

Gil shook his head in disbelief, but he didn't deny that it was possible either. "It couldn't have been Hannah, though," Gil said, shaking his head. "We never . . ."

"What about other girls?" I asked.

"Oh God . . ." Gil turned pale. "Krystal."

"Who's Krystal?" I asked.

"My first girlfriend, the love of my life. That son of a bitch."

"So, are you in?" I asked Gil and Stan.

"Well, I don't have the grudge that Gil here has, but yeah, I'm in all the same. I've got a connection, too. She wasn't the love of my life, but I really liked her . . . a lot." *How many have there been?* I thought to myself. *Does Raymond even know?*

I went back outside where Raymond was deep in conversation with a girl whose name I didn't know. It looked like she was angry and he seemed relieved to see me for once. I motioned to him and he quickly walked over to me as the other girl stared angrily after him.

"Here, Raymond," I said. "You look a little sleepy, take a few more of these. But don't let anyone see you—we're running low."

I handed Raymond the pills, our backs turned to the group, and he greedily shoved them into his mouth without even looking.

Stan took the boat and the rest of our group over to the island while Geena and I got the bartender to call the others on his walkie-talkie.

"Tell them to bring the girls. I got a better deal for them," I told him.

When the gang showed up fifteen minutes later, Raymond was a puddle on a pool table. Completely out of it. Just as I knew he would be, not having any tolerance at all for Benzos. It was just dumb luck that the gang also sold Xanax to help their meth-head customers with those awful comedowns.

We probably hadn't needed to tie him up with the bike locks, but I wanted to. Just for fun.

The bikers brought in Hannah and the other girl. They looked at me with shock, and then even more so when they saw Raymond tied up in bike locks on the pool table.

"So what's this about a better deal?" a guy with a large bushy beard asked Gil, giving me a sideways glance.

"Actually, I'm the one with the offer to make," I said, stepping forward a little, closing the distance between myself and the five bikers. "I have something you can sell that'll never run out . . . if you take good care of it, that is." I smiled and gestured to the pool table, where drool was starting to drip from Raymond's mouth.

At first they didn't believe me, about Raymond having some sort of sexually transmitted plague defense. Once the two girls in their company, as well as Geena and myself, all told them how we all were fine and we had all had sex with Raymond, they were more inclined to believe us.

"Besides," I said, "we're not scientists. We don't know for sure how often or how much we need to sleep with him to keep ourselves safe." I was pretty sure once was enough. But I had learned that the best way to convince someone to do what you want is to prey on their fears. Thanks, Raymond.

"You would have the very source of wellness itself, on tap—for a price of course." I pointed to the girls.

The leader looked at them and at Raymond and back at me and asked me the question I had been waiting for.

"If you're his wife, why aren't you wanting to keep him for yourself, to keep yourself well?"

I looked at him straight in the eyes and said, "Because after the last twenty-four hours, after all the cheating and lying and bullshit he's put me through, I'd honestly rather die of the plague than have his rotten dick inside of me one . . . more . . . fucking . . . time."

As they loaded Raymond up on one of their bikes, slung like a sack over a biker babe's lap, I saw his eyes open a little and a look of brief confusion on his face before he was sucked back into oblivion. It was a state I no longer craved nor cared for.

We all watched as they rode off with their cure, our cure. We had to be grateful for that, at least. Hannah stood there until they were out of sight, her arms crossed, watching with satisfaction, then turned and went back into the bar. She was going to see about staying on as a waitress. I had to admit I was glad she wouldn't be coming with us. Stan honked the boat horn and we soon climbed aboard the little pontoon, ready to start our new life on Gil's island.

"So . . . you don't feel bad about this? Not even a little?" Gil asked me.

"Oh, it's not so bad for Ray. I talked to the guys about the details of the thing and he's just going to have sex with the women in the group who are willing to, so in a way it'll be just like his normal life. They said they'd bring him back to us in a few months once they were sure everyone was inoculated, so to speak. Knowing how much he likes meth and sex with random girls, I doubt he'll even want to come back."

"Everybody ready?" Stan asked.

"Yeah, but one thing's first. I want to drive the boat once we get clear of the Marina," I said.

"Sure, that's fine, but have you ever driven a boat before?" Gil asked, not unkindly.

"Nope, not even once." I smiled. "But I'm a real fast learner."

DAY 3658

Dylan Siegler

"One of us should learn to drive," Zacky said.

"How hard can it be?" Ashley replied. "You just use your feet for the pedals and steer, right?"

"Even if one of us could drive, we'd have a hard time finding a car that works that the military hasn't taken yet," Mandy pointed out. "Not to mention we'd have to constantly look for more gas."

"Ah. Good point," Ashley said.

"Well, fuck, so we're just gonna keep biking forever?" Zacky asked. "We've been at this all day for six days! How are you two not exhausted?"

"Dude, chill out. Biking's good for you," Ashley said. She turned to Mandy. "Biking's good for you, right?" she asked.

"Yeah, it is," Mandy answered.

"Actually, you know what's *really* good for you?" Zacky said. "Not being stuck in a fucking zombie apocalypse."

"True, true," Ashley responded.

"Any kind of apocalypse, really," Mandy said.

"What if, instead of zombies, we were living through a robot apocalypse?" Ashley asked.

"Oh, we'd all be fucked," Zacky answered.

"Why's that?"

"Because robots can have supercomputer intelligence," Zacky explained. "We've all survived this long because zombies are stupid as shit. If they were robots, we'd all be dead."

"I think it depends on the robot," Mandy said. "I mean, not *all* robots are smart, right?"

"I don't know, I think I could take a robot," Ashley said.

"No you couldn't," Zacky responded.

"Uh, yeah I could. Remember when I stabbed that guy when we escaped the Sanctuary? I'm fuckin' lethal."

"What if they're knife-proof robots?"

"Pft, knife-proof robots? Don't be ridiculous."

"Guys, look!" Mandy suddenly said, stopping her bike.

Ashley and Zacky braked and looked in the direction Mandy was pointing and saw what appeared to be a wild dog.

"That's a fuckin' dog," Ashley said. "I'm gonna go pet it."

"Wait, hold on," Zacky said.

"What?"

"What if it bites?"

"Dude, we might never see a dog again!" Ashley pointed out. "I'll risk it."

She dropped her bike and made her way over to the dog, quickly followed by Mandy. Zacky reluctantly came along as well.

Ashley slowly approached the dog.

"Heeeeeeyyy, buddy," she said, reaching her hand out to it.

The dog licked Ashley's hand. She proceeded to pet it. Mandy began petting as well.

"Zacky, come on!" Ashley said.

"What if it has fleas?" Zacky asked.

"God damn it, Zacky, pet the fuckin' dog."

Zacky hesitantly approached and pet the dog.

Mandy was smiling widely.

"Did you use to have a dog?" Ashley asked her.

"Yeah, when I was really little," she answered. She saddened a bit. "We had to leave her behind when the outbreak started."

"That sucks. Sorry."

"I had a cat," Zacky said. "Cats do weird shit."

Mandy laughed. "Like what?"

"I don't know, like freeze up and then start spazzing out."

"Zacky, I think your cat was just dumb," Ashley said.

"It was actually pretty entertaining."

Zacky was the first to look up and see what was approaching.

"Guys!" he said to the other two. "A car!"

"Shit!" Ashley responded. "Is it from the Sanctuary?"

They quickly looked around for a place to hide, but the car drove up to them before they could find one. They turned back and saw there was just one person in it. He stepped out and started towards them. He didn't appear to be wearing military garb.

"There you are!" he said.

Ashley drew her pocketknife and pointed it at the man. "What do you mean, 'There you are?'"

The man put his hands in the air but remained calm. "Whoa, hold up. I was talking to the dog."

Ashley slowly lowered her knife.

"Here, boy!" the man said. The dog ran over to him. He got the dog in the car and turned back to the group. "Are you three out here all alone?"

"We're not alone, we have each other," Ashley answered.

"Okay, fair enough," the man responded. "I'm from a larger group. We have a settlement set up with quite a few people. We have crops and livestock and we haven't had a problem with zombies, or outside people for that matter, in years. You're welcome to come with me back there, if you like."

The group huddled.

"Something seems weird about this," Ashley said. "It's too much like the promises of the Sanctuaries ten years ago."

"Except most of the Sanctuaries are history and these guys are still around ten years later," Zacky said. "Maybe they have some secret to survival the Sanctuaries didn't."

"If most of the Sanctuaries set up by the fucking *military* couldn't make it this long, then how do you not find it suspicious that *this* dude is still alive?" Ashley asked.

"I think it's worth checking out," Mandy said. "If you still feel weird about it after we've looked around, we can leave."

"What if they don't *let* us leave?" Ashley asked.

"Hey, you!" Zacky called out to the man. "If we go with you now, do we have your word that we can leave if we don't like what we see?"

"Of course!" the man replied. "We're not like the Sanctuaries; we don't force anyone to stay against their will."

"Oh, well now I feel much better," Ashley said sarcastically.

"They have a dog that they haven't killed for food," Mandy pointed out. "How bad can it be?"

Ashley was silent for a moment. "Fine. We'll check it out."

They walked up to the man.

"My name's Kevin, by the way," he said. "And that's Rusty." He pointed to the dog.

"How old is he?" Mandy asked.

"He's twelve years old."

"Wow, that's pretty old for a dog."

"Yup, but he's still going strong. He's a little troublemaker too; this isn't the first time he's run away."

"How have you managed to keep him alive?" Zacky asked. "I haven't seen any animals in years. Even all the livestock in the Sanctuary we came from died off a while ago."

"He's like family to us. We take care of him as well as we do our people. So what are your names?"

"Oh, right! I'm Mandy."

"Zacky."

Ashley was silent.

"That's Ash," Zacky answered for her.

"A little skeptical, huh?" Kevin said. "I know, it seems too good to be true, right? I'd be skeptical too if I were in your position."

"Don't mind her," Zacky said.

"'Don't mind her,'" Ashley quietly muttered to herself. "That's what's always said about the skeptic who ends up being right."

"Well, we better get going," Kevin declared. "It's not always safe out here. But I'm sure you three know that better than I do."

Ashley walked back over to where she had dropped her bike and stood it back up.

"Uh, we'll bike along behind you, if you don't mind," Mandy suggested.

"Yeah, sure," Kevin said. "Even if you end up staying, bicycles can be pretty useful. Won't have to keep looking for gas for this thing."

Kevin got in his car and Ashley, Mandy, and Zacky got on their bikes. As they rode, they looked out at the wasteland the Earth had become over the past decade. Plants were few and far between, let alone animals. Buildings were burnt out and crumbling as they passed through the deserted city. The sky was a perpetual gray.

After a few minutes, they reached the settlement.

"It may not be as big as a Sanctuary," Kevin said as he parked his car and got out, "but we're getting by."

As the four of them walked into the settlement's entrance, a kid maybe eleven or twelve ran up to them.

"You found him!" the kid said, petting Rusty.

"Yup. He didn't make it too far this time," Kevin replied.

The settlement seemed to have about fifty people. Most were adults, but there were a few kids about the age of the one petting Rusty. Looking around, Ashley noticed that most of the women appeared to be pregnant.

"Lots of pregnant chicks," she remarked.

"Yup. We make sure they keep those babies coming," Kevin said.

"We used to live in a Sanctuary," Mandy explained, "and they would kill people for getting pregnant. They thought babies just take up space and resources."

"Well, we certainly don't kill people for getting pregnant here."

"You don't think that's weird?" Ashley whispered to Mandy.

"What?" Mandy asked.

"He says they 'keep babies coming,' but there's no babies or really young kids around here."

"They probably have a daycare or something."

"Come on, I'll give you a tour of the place," Kevin said.

They followed him to a large building. When they entered, they noticed quite a few babies and toddlers, all of them appearing to be around or under the age of one. There were a few adult supervisors.

"You see?" Mandy said to Ashley. She turned to Kevin. "We were just talking about where you kept this place."

"Well, here it is," Kevin said.

"Why're they all naked?" Ashley asked.

Kevin laughed. "They're babies, I don't think they mind."

"You really feel the need to question everything, don't you?" Zacky said.

Ashley didn't respond.

They exited the building and entered a slightly smaller one next to it.

"This is our dining hall, of sorts," Kevin said.

"It looks like a high school cafeteria," Zacky remarked. "I mean that in a good way."

"Yeah, this definitely outclasses what we had at the Sanctuary," Mandy added.

As they walked through the dining hall, passing people smiled at them as they carried trays of meat and various fruits and vegetables.

"If you were out of livestock for years, then what did you do for protein? Did you grow beans or nuts or something?" Kevin asked. "If you don't mind me asking."

"We were actually low on crops most of the time too," Mandy replied as her tone depressed. "We actually... sometimes we had to eat the corpses of other people who had already died of hunger. It... we just..."

"That's okay," Kevin interrupted. "You don't have to tell me anymore if you don't want to."

They exited the dining hall and continued the tour. Their next stop was the largest building in the settlement.

"This is where Randal, our mayor, lives," Kevin said as they entered. "It doubles as both his house and office. All residents are welcome to come and go as they please."

"Does one guy really need a house this big?" Ashley asked.

"Ash, for Christ's sake—" Zacky began.

"No, it's all right," Kevin said. "We all have good housing here. We decided as a community that whoever's in charge should have the biggest, nicest house. A perk for handling that much responsibility."

They made their way to Randal's office, which had its door open.

"Hey, Randal," Kevin said as they entered.

"Ah, Kevin!" Randal replied, looking up from his desk. "Giving the tour to some new recruits? It's been a while."

"Well, let's not call them 'recruits' yet. They still haven't made up their minds."

"Well, we'll just see about that by the end of the tour." Randal gave a wide smile.

"They escaped from a Sanctuary and were out alone when I found them."

"No kidding." Randal's facial expression took a serious turn. "I was in a Sanctuary too, at first. I managed to get out towards the beginning. If it was worth escaping from back then, I can only imagine how much worse it was by the time you three escaped."

"Yeah, it... it wasn't great," Mandy replied.

"It was bullshit," Zacky said.

"I'll bet," Randal responded. "I'm sure you'll find our settlement much more favorable. Feel free to stop by any time if you have any questions or suggestions. By the way, what are your names?"

After introductions, they left Randal to work and continued on their way.

They finished the tour, looking at the other places in the settlement and meeting new people, all of whom seemed sincerely nice. By the end, Ashley still wasn't sure about it.

"Something seems off," she said.

"Ash, come on," Zacky said.

"It seems pretty good to me," Mandy said. "Maybe we can stay for a few days and if you still don't like it we can leave."

"Maybe..." Ashley said.

"We can't leave!" Zacky said. "Out there it's hell and this is a paradise! I'm not gonna leave just because you think 'something seems off.'"

Ashley thought for a moment.

"Hey, Kevin," she said. "You said you had crops and livestock."

"Um, yeah," he said, slightly confused. "The crops are all around us." He pointed to various fields around the settlement.

"What about the livestock?"

Kevin was now even more confused. "What do you mean? You saw where we keep the livestock."

Now Ashley, Mandy, and Zacky were confused.

"You even said you were talking about it before I showed it to you," Kevin said.

A wave of shock flew over the group as they realized what this meant. Mandy vomited and almost collapsed. Ashley grabbed her and held her up.

"We're going," Ashley said.

"Are you sure?" Kevin asked.

Ashley helped the sickened Mandy walk and the three of them hurriedly left the settlement. They walked their bikes until Mandy felt well enough to ride again.

"Holy fuckin' hell," Zacky said once they were relatively far away.

"What is wrong with those people?" Mandy asked.

"Well, I don't wanna say I told you so..." Ashley said.

"Ash, I'm so sorry," Zacky said. "I will never doubt you again."

"Damn right you won't!"

"How can they live with themselves?" Mandy went on. "I understand being desperate for food, but... just... oh my god!"

"Let's not think about it," Ashley suggested.

"Good idea," Mandy agreed.

They biked on for a while without speaking.

"How did you know?" Mandy eventually asked.

"What do you mean?" Ashley replied.

"You were suspicious the whole time, even when it seemed there was no reason to be. How'd you know about *this*?"

"I didn't know about *that*," Ashley answered. "I don't know, I'm just skeptical by nature, I guess."

"You weren't skeptical about the dog earlier. Zacky's right, it could have bitten you or—"

"That was a dog, Mandy. Not a person."

Zacky tapped Mandy on the shoulder. She turned to him and he subtly shook his head, signaling that she should not press on. They continued to bike in silence.

Having renewed their distrust in humanity, the group eventually made their way to a new abandoned building to stay the night in and hoped they would have a more productive morrow.

SHELTER

Cynthia Marts

1.

It was twelve past two and I was supposed to be at work at one-thirty. Izaac should have been back an hour ago.

My boots squeaked in short bursts as I paced. I'd been late before, when a wreck on the overstate shut down the outer neighborhoods. A lot of us got in trouble that day. It was made clear that it wouldn't be forgiven a second time.

Now it was so late they'd probably already filed the dismissal paperwork. I'd probably get a phone call in an hour to inform me of my termination, then another from the Department of Women's Services reminding me that a career change meant I'd have to re-file my Transportation and Needs paperwork.

No work meant no reason to travel. It meant no gas rations and barely enough transit slips to get to the store. It meant they'd send pamphlets to my house every week, reminding me of the many religious centers where I could apply for medical, financial, and spiritual services.

Not getting to work in the next fifteen damned minutes meant another string of months confined to my house, my neighborhood, my brother's church. Even walking to the grocery store would require passing a checkpoint.

Izaac needed to get home *now*.

It was six when the phone rang.

The Health and Families attendant was appropriately courteous and spoke with a soft, apologetic tone. They said I could pick up Izaac's personal belongings the following workday, and his car would be placed in storage until a licensed male driver could retrieve it. I peeled at a crack in the wallpaper, my eyes unfocused. I hadn't breathed since the phone rang.

A damage assessment would be sent to my household file once the incident report was finished.

If I felt unsafe alone, I could request a Guardian at any time. If I did not have a designated Guardian one could be provided for me. Did I understand?

I slammed my fist into the wall and took a deep breath.

"I understand."

They thanked me for my time, and apologized for my loss.

 2.

Two weeks later I was in the charity line at the civic center, hoping for a chance at donated gas rations so I could convince someone to get Izaac's car back from the city.

"Donna," someone said behind me.

A young man with slick hair and torn jeans was frowning at me. He was standing behind me, but to my left, not in the line itself.

"Idra?" I asked.

"Donna—" he hesitated, "I heard about your brother."

My eyes were hot as I met his gaze. Idra Parker had been my lab partner in college, up until I was removed.

"I'm really sorry," he said.

I swallowed and turned away again. "Thanks."

The line felt just as long as it had a moment ago, and many moments before that.

What was Idra doing in the charity line? He wasn't just a man, he was rich, too—family money and a lot of it—he didn't need transit or food rations.

I turned further toward him. I hadn't noticed the man beside him, but it was Trenton Jones. He'd lived in the housing block beside mine for years. He was a few years older than Idra and I, but he was living at home after being pulled from a tech university. Now he stood in gas lines so he could give his mother enough rations to work inside the city proper. With a man's ration of gas she could get to the good side of town and find better work; make better money. In the meantime, Trenton walked to work, two miles away.

And here he was, and Idra stood beside him. I noticed their interwoven fists held close between them. Something that had been tight and angry in my chest softened.

"How are you?" I asked Idra, hoping a change in tone could make up for my shortness.

There was a slight quirk of his lips.

"Doing okay," he said, and I could see his fingers tighten a little around Trenton's. It was a gesture, not meant for me, of reassurance or comfort. "But... Where are you?"

I fought a sudden, trembling urge to cry.

"My cousin is putting me up in a few weeks," I said. "He has a spare room. I'm just at the Center for now. Since they, you know... took the apartment."

He nodded, as if it was the answer he'd expected.

"It's not so bad—" I started, as Idra said, "Look, Donna..."

We both stopped.

"Donna, I'm glad we ran into you," he said quickly, his voice low. He pulled a ball of crumpled paper from deep in his pocket and rummaged through receipts and gum wrappers. "There's this place..."

He pushed a slip of paper at me, his eyes on mine. "Trent found it. I think... I think you should look into it."

I watched the hand in front of me, glanced at Trenton and his wide brown eyes, then back at Idra. Was he asking me to take some kind of job?

Was this a risk?

Did it matter?

There was a look on Trenton's face I couldn't explain, but it was determined and sad and it pushed my hand forward.

Paper crunched against my palm.

"Don't... don't tell anyone, you know?"

I clenched my fist.

"Yeah. I know," I said, then paused.

"Thank you," I added.

Idra didn't look at me, but gave a curt nod. "Good luck."

The paper was a crumpled photograph of a house. I recognized it as a women's shelter in the south side. It wasn't well-known, but I'd spent some time there after my parents' death. On the back was a typed passage:

"How wrong it is for a wo**m**an to expect the man to bu**i**ld the worl**d** she wa**n**ts, rather than to create **it** her**s**elf."

The words made chest clench, as if the words had been yanked from my own ribcage. "Feminism" was a dirty word that I had been warned against. This sounded something like it.

Some of the letters were just slightly darker than the others and. On their own, they spelled '**midnite**.' It wasn't very cryptic, but it was all done in such a bland, haphazard way that, for all intents and purposes, one could just glance at the crumpled bit of paper and not notice a single thing peculiar about it.

 3.

For a while I forgot the crumpled photo, and that little tingle of understanding I'd gotten from the words on it.

It wasn't easy to be out after a certain hour without a Guardian. In the past, I'd been asked if I needed someone to walk me home, or how much I cost. It could get much worse for girls after dark, and I'd seen it, but still I wanted to scream at the men, hit them, ask them how much *their* body cost.

But I never got close.

Women aren't allowed to show strength, and there would always be repercussions. So women who are alone stay home. Because just being outside is a risk we're tired of having to take. But the night I moved into my cousin's house, just five blocks from the building in the photograph, I decided to risk the trip.

The shelter had seen better years. When I was a teenager, it still had a playground behind the house and a sign out front that said it was a place of peace. Now the sign was rotting under an empty flower bed, the playground torn out and paved over. Even the mailbox had been pushed over. But it was the same place.

I watched from across the street for a while, waiting. Eventually, two women passed the house, shuffling along the sidewalk together. They paused at the steps while one straightened the crooked mailbox. They stood for a moment, looking around, then slipped across the threshold of the building. It was five till midnight.

When I knocked gently at the door a tall woman in torn work overalls opened it.

"Can I help you?"

I stuttered an "um, I...have...um..." before pulling the photograph from my pocket. She glanced at it, read the text, looked me over.

"You know Trenton?" She asked.

"Sort of. I know his..." I hesitated, "...friend. How did you know?"

I tried to see past her but black curtains shielded everything behind her.

"Everyone has a different quote," she said, holding up the photo, "like a signature. So we know who sent someone. Trenton loves Nin. Did he tell you what this is about?"

"Not at all," I answered.

"Did you lose someone recently? Family, or a husband?"

My throat was dry. I nodded. "My brother."

She nodded back.

"What do we call you?" she asked

"We?"

She didn't respond, but waited, brow raised.

"Donna," I said finally. "Pier."

"Donna Pier, I'm Sasha. Come in."

She took a step back, allowing me to slip past her and the drapes. Inside was a large open space, folding wooden chairs scattered around the room in something like a circle. A handful of people took up just less than half of them, drinking from paper cups and talking quietly. The pair I'd watched outside were sitting near the wall, politely avoiding everyone else's gaze.

I turned to Sasha again. She was locking the door and tying the curtains closed tight. My stomach flipped.

"So, what *is* this about?" I asked.

She smiled, a sort of matronly smile that might have translated to great bedside manner if she could ever have been a doctor.

"This," she gestured around the room, "is a resource. For you, for us, for people who need it. We meet at midnight most nights of the week and we work together to solve things.

"You... solve mysteries?"

She laughed. "We solve *problems*. For each other."

There was a streak of grey running through her hair, like a ribbon of silver that caught the light. I tried to smile with her, but my skin was trembling. I don't know what I'd been expecting, but now my stomach clenched with nerves.

Sasha glanced at a young girl with a surgical boot on one leg, laughing with a blond in a plain cotton dress. She waved, still talking to me.

"Last month we got Cierra a real boot, instead of the broken plastic splint they gave her when they took off her cast at the hospital. There she was limping around and they're all 'sorry ma'am but he needs it more than you' and gives the last of the equipment to the guy *because* he's a guy. They made sure her leg had set and just wrapped it with a splint, then sent her home. I mean, how in the world?"

"How'd you do it?" I asked. I'd forgotten my nervousness by the time she finished.

"Gem's brother is a med student. Hooked us up with a real walking boot that would support her weight and everything. Do you want something to drink? Water? Coffee? Tea?"

"Coffee would be amazing."

She handed me a cup and gestured to a set of carafes.

"Help yourself. We begin when Evee gets here."

"Who's Evee?"

"El Capitan," she said with a grin.

I stood awkwardly by the drinks table, sipping warm black coffee. It made me think of Izaac, and I eventually found a place to sit against the wall, so if I cried maybe no-one would notice.

"I'm here!" someone gasped as they burst through the curtains. "Sorry I'm late."

Evee was a whirlwind of colors and energy, pouring tea into a mug while flipping through sugar packets, talking absently.

"Did you start?" Evee asked.

"No, not yet," Sasha said, bolting the door and drapes again.

"Well, hello friends and new faces. I see a lot of new face, so we'll introduce ourselves to get started this time. Support-group style. Cierra, you know how it goes. Get us going."

The one in the cast grinned. "Hey y'all. I'm Cierra. I work at a haberdashery uptown. Well, I did, til I broke my leg. Now I'm just at home for a while. With my husband. He won't really let me leave, so Gem, here," she gestured to the blond across from her, "brings me to these things when they can."

The two grinned at each other, then Cierra went on, her tone less amused.

"My dad had a temper, now my husband has a temper, and now my leg is effed up because of it. It isn't okay anymore. So. I'm here to help. And I'm here to be helped."

"Thanks Cierra," Evee said, now seated. "Next?"

Someone near the door raised their hand.

"My name's Mickey. I'm pretty new. I'm a mechanic in my brother's shop. I mean, only he knows that I actually fix the cars. Everyone else thinks I'm just the secretary that gets dirty sometimes. But I wouldn't give it up for the world. There's not much I have, but I'm here to help."

"Good," Evee said. "I'm Evee, I run this shindig thanks to Sasha's generosity. I support myself working as a book binder at the warehouse in the new block up north. I identify as female, hate western music, and like to play chess. I'm here because I defy gender norms and sexual norms and lifestyle norms and we all need to have a place to be our damn selves for a change. So. I'm here to help, and I'm here to be helped. Next."

The woman with Mickey spoke up. "I'm Thiu. I live with my parents. I... had a hard time with my ex, and now I'm looking for a new community. I'm doing okay right now, I think, so...I guess I want to help."

I raised my hand.

"My name is Donna, I... used to work at a food distribution center in the suburbs. Then my brother died, and it was just me and him 'cause my parents died years ago, but now he's gone, and they took our apartment, and our car, and I was staying at the Hermia shelter but I just moved into my cousin's place. I guess I'm here for help. I mean, if I can help anyone, I'd like to do that too, I just don't think I have anything to offer." I stopped to catch my breath.

"Thank you, Donna," Evee said with an affectionate smile. "We all appreciate that. Is there anyone else who wants to introduce themselves?"

After the rest of the introductions, Evee put out the call for requests.

"How is everyone? Do you need help? Do you know someone who does? Speak up, folks."

Thiu raised her hand, "My sister's husband just left her and she's been having trouble feeding her family without him. Is there something we can do?"

Evee glanced at Sasha, who nodded. "We can arrange for a delivery this weekend. It won't be much because it's all donation based and the regulations about what people can donate have gotten pretty crazy, but it should help. Does she work?"

"She's been looking for a job since he left," Thiu answered.

"Good," Evee said, "We'll see if we can get some leads for her. Cierra, do you think you could have that friend of yours send some necessities her way?"

Cierra thought about it. "Yeah, but not for another two weeks when Scott's out of town again."

"That'll have to do. If anyone else has ideas, please speak up."

Nobody did, so Evee promised to see what else she could work out, and moved on to a woman in the back of the room who needed medicine for her kids. The rest of the two hours went by similarly, with everyone offering what they could for each other or working out ideas. The overarching theme seemed to be that things sucked for everyone, one way or another. But the more I listened, and the more help and suggestions were offered, the more it also felt like... we could get through it.

In the end, we left one or two at a time, as quiet as possible in the darkness.

On my way out of the neighborhood the sky was a pale blue-grey, dawn not far away. I saw Cierra sitting on a bus stop bench alone. She was fidgeting with a cell phone, playing a puzzle game. I eyed her oversized boot. I didn't want to leave her there alone, so I sat down beside her. We smiled -- somewhere between awkwardness and cordiality.

"I thought Gem brought you," I offered as an ice breaker.

"Gem had to rush straight home — got sick, I think. It happens sometimes. But I still have a copy of my work permit and I know this route driver, so I can hop a bus during certain hours. You?"

"My cousin's place is kind of close, so I'm just walking."

Cierra nodded.

"Did your husband actually break your leg?" I asked suddenly.

She frowned, then shrugged. "Kind of. I mean, I dunno if he meant for me to fall *down* the stairs, just push me back a step. I think the fall was just a bonus. The fucking doctor thought it was funny."

"That's disgusting."

Cierra shrugged again, with a sigh that said she was used to such behavior.

"Ever been married?" she asked after a while.

I shook my head. "Izaac was pretty protective after our parents died. And we were too busy surviving to worry about families or anything."

"That's lucky."

"Lucky?"

"Sorry," she said, "I just meant the single part."

She watched my face, thinking.

"I meant.... You're lucky to be your own person," she said after a moment. "To be free, I guess."

I didn't feel free. I felt alone. I almost said so but she was shifting in her seat, propping her leg, with its hulking plastic cocoon, up onto the bench across from us. Maybe I was lucky in some ways, just not the ones I thought mattered at the time.

The next week, I went to another meeting. Then two the following week. Before I knew it, I felt like maybe I belonged.

A few weeks later the phone rang in the darkness of the early morning. In my cousin's home, all non-essential electricity was shut down at midnight. I'd been pacing the length of my room, fighting a wave of hopeless depression. The horrible blaring ringing snapped me out of a daze. It stopped suddenly, then there were footsteps in the hall.

Neil knocked gently but opened the door right away, frowning at me.

"There's someone on the phone for you," he said. "It's okay this time, but in the future I'd rather you didn't have social calls after dark."

My jaw was clenched tight. "Who is it?" I asked through my teeth.

He shook his head. "Didn't say. Am I understood, though?"

"Yeah, sorry. It won't happen again."

"Fine. Just be quick about it and be quiet. Don't wake Genie up." He handed me the phone and left.

"Hello?" I said.

"Donna?" asked a trembling voice.

"Cierra?"

Over the line, I could hear her sniffling and taking short, gasping breaths.

"Cierra, are you okay?" I asked, then lowered my voice a little more. "What's wrong?"

"Donna.. Something happened... I don't..." her voice broke, "I didn't know who to call. I don't know what to do. I... I'm afraid, Donna."

"What's going on? Where are you?"

There was a lot of sniffling, then coughing, then a seething sound, like air being pushed through teeth. She sounded like she was in pain.

"I'm in the attic. I'm locked in. I know I shouldn't have called you but Gem wasn't answering and I just..."

"It's okay," I whispered, "It's really okay. Here to help, remember? Where is Scott?"

"I heard the door slam, and I think he went out, but I'm not sure and I'm afraid to go check and I don't know what to do."

"Cierra," I said firmly, "where do you live?"

There was a pause, like she had to think about it.

"65 North Court Circle."

Shit. I'd forgotten that Cierra's husband was rich—North Court was two checkpoints away and I definitely wouldn't have any legit ways to get there.

"Okay," I said finally. "Okay. Just... stay where you are. I'm going to hang up now, and I'm coming to get you. Okay?"

Another sniffle, then a strained cough. "Okay."

"Good. Stay put, I'll see you soon."

"Okay."

"Donna?"

I lifted the phone back to my ear. "Yeah?"

"I'm sorry," she said with a choked sob. "I'm sorry I called so late and—"

"Don't you dare apologize," I said, but my voice was trembling. "You're not apologizing for you, you're apologizing for him, and don't you fucking dare. I'll see you soon."

I spent an hour creeping through backyards and tiny dirt roads the whole way to North Court. Izaac and I had spent our pre-teen years exploring the parks and wild green spaces throughout the city before our parents died and things got bad, and it wasn't as hard as I expected to find paths around the checkpoints.

At the last minute, as the first bit of sunrise peeked over the trees, I realized I hadn't thought about how to get *into* the house. But despite the security cameras and a very ornate gate, the back door was unlocked. I ran for the stairs and found the attic door.

"Cierra, it's me," I whisper-shouted at the ceiling.

There was a rumble of motion and something scraped against the wood. Then it opened and Cierra was there with a puffy red face, a black and purple bruise blooming on her temple and a chunk of skin missing from her cheek. Her lip was split and bleeding in two places and her whole body was shivering.

"Holy shit, Cierra."

"He's never done this before, I swear," she said, her voice frantic. "It's never, ever been this bad."

"I don't care. We're leaving. Where's the ladder?"

"There isn't one."

"What? How did you get up there?"

"I was a gymnast," she said with a humorless laugh. She was lowering herself to the floor with just her hands. "Before we got married, Scott was my coach. After, well... he couldn't be my husband *and* my coach. So I became his wife while he got to keep his career. But..." she touched down carefully on her good leg and let out another laugh more like a cough, "I still have great upper body strength."

"I hope you used it to beat the shit out of him."

Cierra flinched and I immediately felt guilty. If she couldn't fight back, there was no shame in it. "Or at least thought about it," I rushed to add.

Her face changed, and she looked both hopeless and angry.

"Every day," she said.

I met her gaze and the blood and bruises made me want to scream, and the idea that the man that was supposed to love her had done this made me want to vomit.

"Come on," I said finally, and offered my shoulder for her to lean on as we limped down the stairs. At the back door, I paused with my hand on the knob. Was that music?

A moment later the door to the garage door swung open and a suited, older man was glaring at us. He smelled like beer and sweat.

"What the hell do you think you're doing?" he asked.

Cierra choked back a word and I cut her off before she tried to speak.

"She needs to go to the hospital."

Scott turned on me. "Who th'fuck are you? What are you doing in my house? Get the fuck out."

"I'll leave, but I need to take Cierra to the hospital. I don't know what happened but her cheekbone looks broken and she's lost a lot of blood. I think she was attacked."

"She isn't going anywhere," he said with a laugh. "Now get out of my house."

He reached for Cierra's arm and I pulled us both back.

"I'm taking her to the hospital. You need to move out of the way."

"Cierra, who is this?"

But Cierra was trembling against me, her jaw clenched so tight I could see the muscles work, hear the grinding of her teeth.

"Sir," I said slowly, "we need to get to the hospital. Move out of the way."

"This is ridiculous," he said, and lunged for her, one hand pushing me away while the other wrapped around Cierra's forearm.

His palm hit me with enough force that I fell backward. Cierra let out a panicked cry and jerked, tripping on her boot.

He stood over her, his face a mask of anger and panic.

"What's going on here, Cierra?" he asked. "What are you doing? Did you bring her here? Into my house? Into our *home*?"

Cierra didn't answer, just crawled backwards, dragging her leg.

"What did you do, Cierra?" he asked again.

"Leave her alone," I said when I was able to stand back up. "We're going to the hospital."

He watched me, seeming bewildered that I'd spoken. "No you aren't," he said carefully. "My wife is staying here where she belongs. Do you know who I am? No doctor will even see her without my permission."

I was horrified by the idea. I stood tall, clenching my fists to keep myself from shaking. I pushed past him and helped Cierra up again. He lunged for us and I lashed out, pushing back against him with my whole body. As if we'd timed it, Cierra hooked her cast behind his ankle, so when he fell back, he fell down. I watched, immobile, as he tripped on the first step into the garage, one leg twisting behind him as he crumpled to the ground, his head hitting the ground with a sick, wet crack.

The adrenaline in my system burst beneath my skin like tiny pin-prick fireworks. Scott was a heap of groaning muscles on the floor, one knee bent at a horrifying angle, blood seeping from the back of his head onto the concrete flooring.

"Shit," Cierra hissed, tears spilling over her cheeks. "Scott—"

"God damn it!" he gasped. "Cici, you're going to regret this. You're never leaving again. You just wait. They'll put you on house arrest for this. Your friend's going to jail for assault. You can't do this to me." He let out an incoherent, rambling groan, then raised himself up on one shoulder, collapsing with a scream when he tried to move his legs.

Cierra lurched forward half a step. "Scott..." she muttered again, but I held her back.

Then his voice was a hushed whisper as his eyes rolled, lids flickering shut. "Gonna... fuckin... regret..."

There was a moments silence, then Cierra let out a strangled moan.

"Oh god," she whispered, "Oh god. What did I do? Is he dead?"

I lost focus for a moment, staring at him, waiting for the rise and fall of his chest. I was on the security cameras. If he died, they'd know if was our fault. With Cierra's wounds, they'd have an idea of why, but that wouldn't matter. We'd both rot in a women's sanatorium, diagnosed with hysteria and convicted of murder.

"Donna!" Cierra hissed, bringing me back from my fear. I went down the steps, but as I reached Scott he sucked in a huge gasp of air, as if he'd been drowning. Cierra and I flinched, but he was still unconscious, and his shallow breathing continued.

"Let's go," I said in a rush of breath. "Out the back."

"But Scott --"

"We need to be gone when he wakes up."

Cierra hesitated. "Is he okay?"

"It doesn't matter. We have to leave. Now."

I pulled her towards the back door.

"Do you have family in the city?" I asked. She shook her head, crying.

"Do you have anywhere you can go?" I pressed. She shook her head again.

"Donna, what do I do?"

I waited, thinking. Outside, the sun was rising over pristine neighborhood trees. We were running out of time.

"Can you make it to Sasha's?" I asked. "Are you okay enough to get there?"

She rubbed her face with her hands, wiping away tears and massaging her cheeks. She took a deep breath and met my gaze. There was a deep, determined strength in her eyes and she nodded. "I can make it."

"I've got to get home," I said said, "so we can split up when we get past the second checkpoint, okay? Then I'll meet you at Sasha's tonight. Just stay there, okay? All day, no matter what. Okay?"

She nodded again. "Okay."

I squeezed her hand, offered her my shoulder again, and we left that horrible man behind.

That night, I snuck out after the lights were out, and found Cierra on the shelter's porch, bandaged up, with her arm draped over Gem's shoulder. Gem was wearing hospital scrubs and had a bottle of water against their belly.

"Are you alright?" I asked.

Gem's eyes were clenched shut, their breath slow and measured. Cierra answered first, pulling me away gently.

"Gem had a procedure last night," she said in a whisper. "I'm not sure they did it right."

I knew the euphemism and didn't press. "Is there anything I can do?"

She shook her head. "I don't think so. Evee will make sure they're okay."

"Is anyone else here yet?" I asked.

"Yeah. They're... discussing."

Inside, Sasha and Evee were arguing while the usual group watched awkwardly. The three of us sat down near the door so we wouldn't interrupt them, and I was immediately fascinated. They knew about Scott, and Cierra's involvement, and mine. And they were talking about doing something insane: leaving.

"You want us to walk across the country?" Sasha was asking, throwing her hands up.

"It's just to the border."

"It's like a hundred miles. That's crazy and it'll never work. You're crazy."

"Look at what's happening to us. Do you have a better idea?"

"Yes! Mickey has a perfectly good plan. You heard her last week! It's a *good plan.*"

"Yeah, a perfectly good plan that would take three months to work. We wouldn't be able to get enough gas rations in the little time we've got."

"So we get an electric. Mickey knows a guy who can get a deal—"

"We would never have enough! We could sooner get a goddamned helicopter, Sasha! We will get *caught.*"

The word "caught" seemed to hover in the air and there was a deep silence. If they did this—if *we* did this—getting caught was not an option.

My throat was dry and my fists clenched. Evee met Sasha's gaze, defiant, and I scanned everyone's faces in the quiet. They all knew the stakes: There were no right answers, and no good choices. I wondered if I had a side in this. Scott was going to come after Cierra, and he was going to come after me eventually, too. He could end us with a handful of the right words. Assault. Hysterical. Tramp. Queer.

My cousin wouldn't protect me from those types of accusations.

"We can't *walk,*" Sasha went on. "Not all of us could even get that far. Gem just had a... a miscarriage for fuck's sake, Cierra is still in a cast and can't go home. What the hell would they do?"

Evee took a deep breath. Gem's expression had darkened when their name was mentioned, and now they met her gaze. She stood her ground and spoke again, each word firm and clear.

"We'd need thirty rations to get one vehicle across the border alone, that's two weeks right there. Gem needs hospital care sooner than that. If Cierra's husband doesn't come after her, her job will. They'll lock Donna up for her part. Always another one less of us. So all this work and only a few of us even get *out*. If it even works at all. Is that what you want?"

Sasha avoided her gaze and stayed silent.

"But we can gather enough food in a few days," Evee went on, "We can get through the city more carefully on foot. We can cover short distances by day, like everybody else, trade the rations we've got to get rides when we can, then go the long distances at night. It'll take two or three days, but that gets us moving and out of the city within a week."

She watched the people around her, then added, slowly, "It's our best option to get everyone free."

Something tingled under my skin like dancing light, and I remembered something Izaac had once said. Something about being free.

No one broke the silence until there was a sudden voice: Mine

"That might not be true," I said before I could stop myself. "I think there's another way."

Evee crossed her arms but waited without speaking. There was a murmur of whispers behind her.

Sasha asked, finally, "Okay, Donna. What is it?"

I stuttered for a moment, my stomach churning. Then I thought about Izaac, and what he would have done.

"Well, we need to get out of the city carefully, without anyone noticing— so we travel quiet—" I gestured to Evee, "—like walking at night. Be we need to go as fast as possible," I motioned again, towards Sasha, "so... cars. But without the rations, gas, money, or city checkpoints. Um... What if we could meet in the middle?"

My eyes flicked around the room. I licked my lips, then spoke quickly. "A while back, before the accident, my brother and me found a transit center buried in the Downs. Like, *buried* buried. There were all these old stores and stuff, but I guess the place was too hard to get to or something, cause none of them had really been looted or anything, so they were all full of stuff, like they were just left alone all this time. It was crazy cool. We played around, you know? Pretending things were open and normal and stuff." I could see Izaac, modeling a rhinestone sweater and lying on a bed of snack-cake boxes.

I shrugged and went on, "We took some stuff, yeah, for our building. Clothes, books, batteries. Some canned food. Toys. Y'know? Anyway there was this one store we couldn't get in to, it was really locked down and the gates were bent up and just strong as hell, but we could see in the windows and stuff, and I think," I paused, licked my lips again, and thought of steel bars and knobby rubber wheels, "I think it was a bike store."

Someone behind Evee let out a short laugh. Mickey's eyes lit up. Sasha's brow creased.

Cierra, who was the youngest, asked slowly, "What's a bike?"

Evee's expression flew through confusion to curiousity, then she grinned. "Something like freedom."

 6.

Beyond the checkpoints and the towers and all the broken down suburbs, the wind hit my cheeks like tiny frozen shards. It blew my hair behind me like twisting willow branches, made my eyes water, my flesh tingle. My breath somehow both burned and froze in my chest, heavy and sharp. The occasional houses in the street were dark, quiet: safe. No one would see us this late, and any that did would only see shadows plummeting down the hill.

I couldn't breathe. I couldn't think. But I could feel.

The wind. The air. The burning in my thighs. The pump of blood in my temples. The grooves of the handlebars under my palm.

Behind me, Cierra lounged in her cart, both arms stretched out like wings. I glanced back once and her eyes were closed, her head titled towards the sky. Ahead, Mickey had paused to adjust the makeshift seat on the back of her bike for Gem, and Sasha was scanning the horizon from her loaded cargo bike. The rest of us flew past silently in the pink dawn light.

Through it all, it was the wind that got me. Like needles against my face. My legs pulsed, throbbed with exhaustion, my back ached from the strange new curve of my spine. The various pains were so wrenching that I wanted to let go; to just drop my legs and collapse onto the unforgiving asphalt.

But there was also this feeling behind my chest, inside of my bones, as if the world were in a vast cavern that existed within my ribcage, breathing inside of me. A deep, humming resonance like a song.

They said it would be something like this, but I hadn't believed them. Or Izaac.

Izaac said it would feel free.

QUESTIONS WITH THE FIRST

Jim Warrenfeltz

Q: –and now the tape is rolling, so we're all set. Alright, I was thinking first some background questions, then get into this year's Race a little bit, perhaps, depending on time, of course, wouldn't want to miss midnight-

A: Ahem.

Q: –I thought that we could–

A: Ahem.

Q: –that we could . . . um. . .

A: I hate to stand on formalities. But. Here we are. Me here. Big chair, big desk, finery and pomp and circumstance. You there. Little chair. Little notebook. Little tape recorder. Of course, I am One of the People and the First Among Equals and everything . . .

(a six-second pause)

(a sound of scuffling feet and chair legs, rustling fabric)

Q: Hail to You, Most Exalted and Supreme First Among Equals!

(a four-second pause)

A: Yes, quite, quite. Thank you. After all, this is for posterity. Please, sit.

Q: Yes, Your Highness.

A: Please, please. You can call me Sam. Would you like a drink? I'm drinking. They say that if you're drinking alone, you have a problem. I wouldn't want something like that to go in your little article, now would I?

Q: Um . . . I'm not sure that–

A: If it will get you to stop sniveling and absolutely *reeking* of fear and flop-sweat and . . . is that nervous flatulence? Call me

Sam, get comfy, have a little drink, whatever it takes. Please. For the sake of my own nasal passages. Don't worry. When your tape is returned, everything on it will be quite proper, to be sure.

Q: Okay. Sam.

A: Fantastic. What a breath of fresh air, as it were. Brandy? Whiskey? I'm having vodka, but only so I can see any of the colored poisons . . .

Q: Uh–

A: Most are clear, of course, but . . . can't be too careful. Perhaps you would care to sample some cognac? And then I could have some.

Q: . . . yes?

A: Good!

Q: Your Hi– Sam, a few background questions. Your early life is shrouded in mystery. There are rumors about–

A: Are there? Well, I certainly haven't heard any. Go on, I am intrigued.

Q: Rumors about–

A: Genuinely intrigued by what possible rumors could exist about me. Of course, there is talk, I am told, that my mother was less than a saint, that my father was absent. Or beat me. Or her. Rumors that my father wasn't known. I have heard those rumors—but only once. We couldn't let such vicious slander spread, could we?

Q: Um. Rumors about–

A: Or could this be about my role in the Tar Sand War? That, of course, is public record, which could be looked up at the Capitol Library quite easily by a talented journalist such as yourself. Why would you bother asking me such things, when of course, your time is valuable; as is mine?

Q: Let's move on to the founding of The People's Republic of Real America.

A: Certainly. Funny story about that, actually. You wouldn't believe how difficult it was to get that name approved.

Q: America?

A: Well, the whole thing. See, back in the day, certain people didn't really approve of the People's Republic part. Others didn't like the Real America part. Nobody's happy.

Q: And what happened?

A: I suggested people get happy.

Q: And that worked?

A: In the long run.

Q: So . . . after the name, you built the Capitol.

A: A fine city, indeed.

Q: Why white marble spires? And why did you choose to build directly in the Rockies, above the tree line?

A: Well, the views are stunning. From both ways, actually. You can see the Capitol across the face of the PRRA on a clear day. And the white marble, the pure white marble, represents the purity of our mission as a people. You wouldn't believe how hard I had to fight on that one, too. Architects said, "Why not granite? The Rockies are already built out of it, you know. Much easier and less expensive than importing marble." They didn't get it.

Q: Get what?

A: I didn't want the Capitol to blend in, to be easy. I want it to loom over the PRRA. Loom may not be the right word there. Let's have another go. I want it to preside over the PRRA, like a father looking over his sleeping children. Keeping them honest.

Q: And then the Third Founding.

A: Right. The People's Republic. The Capitol. And.

Q: The Race.

A: Most people don't try to steal my lines. Don't worry, though. I like you. Now try some of the bourbon, please. Tell me if your lips burn. Or go numb. Tinnitus is another symptom.

Q: How did you come up with the idea for The Race?

A: When times are tough, people need an example of how hard work, sacrifice, and struggle can take the common person and elevate them to the role of the Hero. In the early years of the PRRA, times were very tough indeed. And your next question, of course, is . . .

Q: Is?

A: Now that times . . .

Q: Now that times . . .

A: Aren't . . . Aren't . . . Aren't t-t-t-toooooooooou-

Q: Oh, right! Now that times aren't tough, what value does the Race provide?

A: Well, in times of plenty and excess, as we live in now, people need entertainment. And, I suppose, examples. Of the dangers of laziness. Vice. Ineptitude.

(tinkling of ice in a glass and pouring sounds)

Q: So the example people are supposed to draw from the Race is that, if you can outlast 99 other people, you can succeed in the PRRA?

A: Hah! No, no, of course not. Here in the PRRA, we are the one percent, we are the successful.

Q: But the Race contestants are drawn from the PRRA youth. By lottery. So in reality, the Race's riders represent us all, surely?

A: Yes. The contestants are drawn completely by lottery. Completely.

Q: You're tapping your nose.

A: And winking, yes. Surely you've noticed that many of the riders represent certain . . . undesirable groups of people. Demonstrate certain traits, certain attitudes that we don't wish to encourage in our grand nation.

Q: Such as Ashanti last year.

A: Who?

Q: Ashanti.

A: Ah, yes, well, we prefer to refer to our riders by their race number, of course, rather than by name. Too much personification of the racers tends to distract the viewers at home from the moral lessons and entertainment.

Q: Alright. Number 98 last year.

A: I know, right? Number 98! She got sooooo close! Believe me, if you can keep a secret, and I know that you can, I was actually rooting for her by that final week. That flat tire on the second-to-last day. So unfortunate. But her bravery! And how she kept pedaling as the clock reached midnight; by the end her rim was bent and she was dragging the bike more than riding it . . . and still, she was only twenty miles short of being Number 99! Or maybe even winning it! And then she could have been in the spot that our wondrous winner Walter is. Have you seen him, Walter, lately?

Q: No, not exactly.

A: The other week I saw him. He was cutting the ribbon at an opening of a new McDonald's here in the Capitol. Smiling and smiling. Still so thin, though. Should spend some time in that McDonald's, right?

Q: So, what traits did Ashanti—Number 98—have that should have telegraphed her downfall to us?

A: Number 98 was prideful. Thought that she knew better than everyone else. Everyone else, including her elders. Her political leaders. Her betters. How can you know better than your betters? Right? It's a contradiction in terms.

Q: Changing gears–

A: Ah-hah! Puns! Very good, very good. Haven't introduced the death penalty for puns yet, have I?

Q: Um . . . To ask a different line of questions—do you have any favorites in the Race this year?

A: Ah, well, can't very well refer to them by number at the moment, can I? Of course, I could tell you about numbers 1 through . . . 18 as of yesterday, right? Unfortunately, none of them were very interesting. 1 was another Conscientious Objector this year, wasn't he? Boring. Ruins the whole first day and is very, very unfair to the viewer at home. Where's the suspense, right, the scramble at midnight? The first couple of weeks, with the poor, untrained paste-legs all trying to scrape out a mere two or three hundred miles a day, those are probably my favorite days. I stay up every night for the day's Grand Finale in the first couple of weeks. When you know who it's going to be for twenty-three hours and fifty-five minutes, it ruins it.

Q: Fifty-five minutes?

A: Well, there's always just the chance that he's frozen with nerves, right? Could find his gumption, blast out and ride two hundred, maybe. But five minutes, that's about when they start trying to do their Speech. Very boring. More bourbon?

Q: Speech?

A: Yeah, they all want to say something to the folks at home. Get people to rise up. As if people could do better on their own than I do for them. It is rough. I'm going to be honest, people do *not* appreciate me at all. If you people only knew.

In any case, those Speeches never go out, of course. Sometimes they even try to do them at midnight, right up to the moment the Sweep Team comes up and Withdraws them from the Race. And then they've gone and ruined both the suspense and the first night's Grand Finale. So disappointing.

Q: So not Number 1.

A: (laughs) No. Not this year, no.

Q: What about the girl, Becca?

A: . . . Becca.

Q: People are comparing her to Ashanti.

A: You know, I could act like I don't know who you're talking about. As if she were beneath my notice. As if I didn't care. But that would be a lie. And the people would know it was a lie, because I do care, and I do notice. Becca is certainly . . . an interesting case. She's almost the exact opposite of a Freezer, isn't she?

Q: Could you elaborate?

A: I mean she certainly hasn't refused to participate in the Race. But most of the contestants will conserve their energy and only put twenty miles up on the hindmost of the day. Ten, even. Walter had a period last race, there was a month where he was only one or two miles up on the hindmost. Very tricky. Recovered, while the rest burnt their selves out.

But Becca. Becca is putting up three, four hundred a day. Becca is going to destroy herself. Becca is going to burn up. Becca is in a dangerous place.

Q: She's doing loops of the Capitol.

A: I know! Don't I know it?! Becca has made it necessary to send a special crew out, solely for her. I get twenty-four hour coverage of Becca, round and round. And–

(rustling sounds, as the recording device is moved, and from this point the voice of the First is much louder, as if the microphone were being held directly to the First's mouth)

–And, I want this to be clear, I see the faces of all the people on the walls of the Capitol. I see you, cheering Becca on. I see who is throwing flowers beneath her wheels. I see everything! Do not think, just because you are Capitol Citizens, that you are immune and untouchable! Do not think so!

I want this printed, and I want it printed very clearly. All of this.

The list of contestants for next year is being drawn up right now. Those of you who are of eligible age would find it very recommendable to withdraw from the walls tonight. Those of you who have children of eligible age. Or who are planning on children. The State, the PRRA, and First, our memories are long and we are unforgiving; we are stern and we are disappointed in each and every one of you!

(deep, heaving breaths)

Q: Alright. Alright?

A: Oh, yes. I'm perfectly alright. I'm still here, aren't I?

Q: Well, it's a few minutes to midnight—and I want to again emphasize how much I appreciate your time–

A: You are quite welcome. I am a very busy person, after all.

Q: –so I wanted to ask if you had any concluding thoughts, before tonight's Sweep Team appearance?

A: Actually, yes, a few.

Citizens of the PRRA, this is your leader, the First Among Equals. You can call me Sam. You know me. You love me. My past is your past, my future is your future. You were born with me, I mid-wifed you into the world.

This Becca, this false idol who you adore. Let me tell you a few things about her.

She is not a symbol of change. She is not a prophet. She is not a leader of a revolution.

She is a teenager on a bicycle. She is not unbreakable. She is not indominatable. She will be broken, she will be dominated by the Race.

So she is an orphan from the streets. So she volunteered for the Race. So she rides like a maniac, round and round, ignoring your cheers, ignoring your jeers.

That doesn't mean she's an inspiration. That doesn't mean that she is an example of silent protest, of beating the system by bettering it.

It simply means that she is an obstinate teenager throwing a tantrum.

Is this your inspiration, your leader, your messiah? A child? I should think not.

I expect more from you, citizens.

Q: The Withdrawal!

A: Ah, midnight. And our new Number 19. Poor girl rode two hundred and sixty-three miles today. Goodbye, Number 19. May the legs that failed you today not fail you in the afterlife.

(a pause and then a hollow bang, followed by somber music)

You press people always do such a good job on the Withdrawals. That one felt like we were right on the road with her. You could see the acceptance and compliance in her eyes. And midnight is such a hard time to light for television, too. Perhaps we should change the time of Withdrawal to noon?

Q: Perhaps.

A: Hmm.

(a muffled chant is heard, low and hard to make out)

A: I'm sorry. I thought I had told my underlings that I wanted this room soundproofed. How embarrassing.

(the chant rises in volume)

Q: What are they saying?

A: That small rabble? I wouldn't know. I expect they think it will disturb my sleep.

(the chant is almost intelligible)

A: I sleep like a baby; I sleep the sleep of the righteous and the just!

(the chant can be made out)

Chant: 503! 503! 503!

(the chant repeats through the end of the recording)

Q: (voice slightly raised) What does it mean?

C: 503! 503! 503!

A: It's nothing. It's stupid. It's both nothing and stupid!

C: 503! 503! 503!

A: It's the number of miles Becca rode today! And it is not inspiring, and it is not impressive, and it is not frightening! She will burn out! She will burn out and die, and she will be a number, and she will be forgotten! And her number will not be 503!

C: 503! 503! 503!

Q: She has eighty more days. It could be higher, Sam.

A: . . . God help us all.

C: 503! 503! 503! 503! 503! 503! 503! 503! 503! 503! 503! 503!

THE FUTURE OF FLIRTATION

Leigh Ward-Smith

In the seven years she'd run the mobile Mika's Grille, through the water riots and rebellions and plague, Mika had developed   serving-customers-while-covering-her-own-ass into a fine art form. It was like a marriage from the days before all hell came crashing down, she'd often thought: to love and honor, for worse and for worser. She'd dug her nails into the generators and other gear and not let go for any man's money. Without it, the diner would've flopped and died—which, incidentally, was what happened to a host of others.

And now here she was, ministering to a dwindling population of nomads and rag-tag survivors. These characters clawed their way out of the dust for just a single morsel, a sole hit, one whiff, or one spliff. Reunited with some forgotten favorite. That, or to make acquaintance with a life form other than heat-seeking reptilians.

If these wanderers were lucky, they had functioning hydrocycles. Otherwise, most people had to make do with their feet or any random animal that could be tamed and ridden to its demise in the heat. Even on more temperate days in what used to be called fall or autumn, the fist-busted outdoor thermometer routinely stretched its red line into the low 90s.

Today, kicking up soiled confetti leading to Mika's place was a figure attached to a hydrocycle. Mika instinctually patted the gun hidden at her hip, hoping for the best but more than prepared for the worst that doomsday could muster. Once stopped, the person didn't remove their helmet, which was an unadorned obsidian-black and had a shimmer effect in the heat. In a dust storm out here in the heat-ravaged elements, she knew such helmets were not just de rigueur. They were literal self-preservatives. *Ha ha, pickled people*, she thought.

Peering around the dark-clad form that was starting to capture her curiosity, Mika could see the impressive cycle, obviously made of cannibalized parts, a quartz homage to kinetic energy. Alongside, riding sidecar, a water-recycling unit.

The visitor swung off the bike and neatly chewed up the distance from the gravel area to the makeshift diner. Mika rubbed the slim .38 for comfort, mentally noting to print some more bullets. Soon. Best to be safe.

Mika had pegged the stranger at a solid six feet or so, just looking at the spiked angles of leather-swaddled legs sitting on the bike, but that estimate grew as the looming form approached on foot, scratching a raspy ostinato through the sediment. 6'3". 6'4". Oh jeez, gotta be at least six-foot-five, maybe a couple above it. Any way you look at it, this character's massive. Mika clamped down the delight shuddering in her ribcage. Depending on the circumstances, she might settle for a sexy, stubbled beast, but she longed for a woman instead. One to make even her teeth sweat. Either way, this one is goddamned sexy. Tall, athletic, self-assured.

"Heard you might have some Coke," a voice came from out of the visor. Obscured from the waist down behind the countertop, the visitor sat heavily. Mika could imagine this stranger's gangly knees hitched up on the other side of the barrier. Knees attached to thighs attached to yielding flesh. She shrugged off the discomfort of not being able to clap her baby browns on another pair of eyes. She wanted to yell, to trill, "Take off the damned helmet and let me get a long-delayed look at you and your goodies."

As if sensing her doubts, the visitor added, "Don't you worry, lady. I ain't here to rob you. In fact, I've got plenty enough ellies." They patted at their left chest, where Mika figured an inner pocket lay. The grace of their carriage and movement was at once tantalizing and scary.

Backing up to the stash, Mika kept her eyes riveted to the mirrored helmet.

She fished the soda out of the cooler-sized refrigerator and sat it down in the circle of Helmet-Head's hands, also black-clad. The hands made her think of a barred metal gate. A through-way she intended to enter. *Persuasion is my forte. Lay it on thick, Mika.*

In Mika's experience, half the haggle instinct was killed by just introducing the sight of the product. That got the mouth watering, the senses jittering. Truth be known, if there was anyone to unload it on, in normal circumstances she craved being the leader in laying out a deal. *Be cool, Mika. I know they'll consent to me being on top.*

Before the visitor could get a hold, Mika snatched it away. She held the frigid can a-dangle. "That'll be 200."

"How about 160?"

She was more than beginning to wonder if the essentially cloaked character in front of her, dark hair lightly curling out from under the helmet, identified as male or female or neither. Moreover, did they go for girls or guys? Or both? Or neither? Even the angular, beefy gloves gave nothing away; either phalanges delicate as fairy floss or trunk-thick masculine knuckles. The voice was alluring, but essentially sexless. *It's been so long . . . too long . . .*

Mika knew she'd have to stop that bad habit of chewing at her lower lip. Best not to seem vulnerable. "Make that 170 and you've got a deal."

"Deal," Helmet-Head mumbled, pulling loosely rolled bills free from their inner jacket, which covered a simple gray T-shirt, pocket partly hanging free. Mika stared but saw no telling body contours whatsoever. Helmet not even looking down, the enigmatic stranger piled seventeen bills on the counter methodically. There was a studied, limber athleticism to the movement of the long, fluid arms that Mika got caught up in or, rather, wished she were.

"Got any more, for the road?" the visitor said, now tilting the can from side to side. Beads of moisture cascaded down the closed can and around their tenacious grasp.

Just to be sure, Mika rapidly blinked a few times, and it seemed the same vision, not any figment. The stranger had gripped the stiff, full container so hard it seemed to be caving in under the gloved fingertips. If Mika had been taller, she would have definitely risked a look-see at the apex of the stranger's narrow pelvis.

"Unh-hunh," Mika mumbled.

"Same price or a discount for an old friend?"

Somehow Mika knew her peculiar visitor didn't smile, either while talking or after. You couldn't be too safe around strangers or other scavengers these days.

Mika tamped down a pang of lust for mysterious wayfarers, cultivated over many a solitary day. "As to the cost, look, you seem like a traveling person, so I'm gonna just put this idea out in the open." Her Rottweilers, Tarja and Zisa, had since padded in quietly, taking a place not too far from her feet, on the thin strip of kitchen floor in the grille, where the tile was beginning to curl up at the edges. She suspected the stranger saw the sturdy canine companions, one of whom had taken to a low whine.

"I'm not much interested in your money. Ya got anything to trade instead?" Mika elaborated, quirking an eyebrow.

"Hafta be more specific than that," Helmet-Head quickly looked down, a gesture Mika thought meant impatience.

Still the stranger clutched the canister. All the while, Mika got caught up in the radiant, dripping can. It was practically sweating around where the leather gloves held it. *Damn, aren't they at least thirsty in this heat? I would be.*

Mika didn't even hide her lip-licking now, imagining the heat tickling the curve of the stranger's lower back. She thought to put a hand on the stranger's glove resting on the counter but held back until the deal was in the clear. Business and pleasure mixed in her previous life experience about as well as sand in a leather thong.

"Any water rations, spare parts . . ." Mika flipped a straggling auburn curl away from her eyes with a head-toss, "bullets, virtual cigs, matches, paperbacks, dimensional printers, uh, sex toys, solar playthings, toilet paper, rations, anything barter-wise. I don't get that many visitors." She had grinned seductively but an immediate thrust of regret speared at her. She glanced down at Zisa to reassure herself. The dog snuffled in the midst of a thin layer of sleep.

"Ah, contraband." Helmet-Head forged right to the point. If it had been her, she probably would have smiled, at least wryly, but this impossibly tall stranger's voice didn't betray a waver. It had a methodical quality, for all the studied patois. "Guess it depends on what you're offering as to what I've got to barter." Mika got the feeling they made calculations, not to mention real-world valuations, atomically fast.

"Well, I might have a whole six-pack of probiotic lager or something attractive I can rummage up," Mika suggested. "If the price is fair."

Helmet-Head rose up off the stool. In a spark, they were ready to hurtle out of Mika's life. "Sorry, miss, I don't need alcohol. But how 'bout that second Coke?"

"Yeah, hang on, just a sec." Against all instinct, Mika whirled to the little unit hidden in the cabinetry and keyed in the code, turning her own back on the mystery person. Didn't somebody once say such confidence was sexy?

She withdrew the can, pausing to scrape the coat of ice from its hull. Then she sat it on the counter and looked up toward Helmet-Head's crown. Their head was now well above the awning and Mika at last caught a glimpse of a muscle-swaddled neck. Lithe and swanlike, but as if that bird were on steroids. *Jee-zus, they're pushin' 6'8" then, and strong as a bear by the looks of it. Swoon.*

"It's on me." Mika surprised herself, wishing that the someone before her would literally be on her, rather than the metaphorical freebie. Would this maddening sexpot of a stranger ever get the hint? Shit, were they even interested at all? Mika figured if the powerful-looking stranger had wanted to, they could've loped over to the bike in five good strides. Or, for that matter, back at Mika to wring her much thinner neck, though she figured the dogs would have something to say to that prospect. Plus, it would fuck-up the soda for a few minutes, if they intended to drink it right away. *I think you're safe, Mika; never mind the lack of bullets.*

"Hey, what'cha need with just two pops out here in the ass crack of the Earth?" Mika still salivated for the stranger's company. The opportunity for an alleviation to boredom and lust was getting more and more distant. Mika's jaw dropped as she watched those blurred edges and a towering black-clad backside—head, trunk, high and firm butt, miles of legs, and all of those luscious bits in between—stride away from her.

Probably forever.

From a distance, Mika saw the mysterious rider press an unseen something on the helmet, raising the visor so only a wraparound rectangle of facade was present.

Then, as if saying cheers, they'd raised the can in Mika's direction, then tipped and downed it. Directly into their right eyeball.

After a few seconds that seemed like forever, Mika grinned to herself, already choosing her diary words, which included, "I'll do things differently with the next alien-robot babe that comes along."

The burr of the bike as the rider accessed its stored energy soon twisted itself up in the anemically rising wind.

Would anyone ever believe the whole eye-porthole thing? I mean, this creature had to come from . . . what, the frekkin' Soda-Pop Planet?

Damn, I hope they come back.

MAAIKE'S AQUATIC CENTER FOR BICYCLES RAISED BY FISHES

Jessie Kwak

Dearie come in, come in. Welcome to the Center. Are you the one that's called ahead, love, looking to adopt a bicycle? Ah, good.

We've about a dozen at the Center most days, give or take. You'll find that some are still slightly skitterish, some bold and playful, and some—oh, sweetheart, I'm sorry, I should have told you. You'll not want to touch our Willa; she's not got her land sense back as such. I'll get you a bandage. There.

It's good of you to come in. Sometimes these ones get no love, these waterlogged bicycles tugged from beds of radiators and shopping carts and strollers and all the other things people throw into the canals. But the Center takes them in, don't we, and it's all thanks to good folks like yourself.

We've a series of pools out back; I can take you if you like. The first pool is just the right combination of sea brine and river silt and engine oil and, well it wouldn't be proper to say what else, but I'm sure you can guess. We had a scientist come and look at it last summer and he says it's as good as canal water any day. The newcomers always start there, where they feel safe.

There's the halfway pools, of course, for those that haven't sorted themselves out yet and still need a dip to ease their rusty joints. But bit by bit our trainers get them out into the open, with cozy towels and superfine sandpaper and grease for their bearings and chains.

Now, sweetie, remind me your inseam? Oh, haven't I got just the little angel for you: a townie with a fresh coat of sky blue paint. You'll like her. She's even taken to fenders and a rack, just as happy as can be. I'll just go fetch her, then.

Nonono, Willa! Sit. Now there's a good girl.

●   ●   ●

Frequently Asked Questions

Thank you for your interest in adopting from Maaike's Aquatic Center For Bicycles Raised By Fishes. Every one of our bicycles is fished from the canals of Amsterdam and lovingly rehabilitated into perfectly well-behaved beasties in need of a good home. We hope this answers your questions, but if not, feel free to ask us anything!

How are the bicycles recovered?

In their heart of hearts, even bicycles raised by fishes know they're meant to zip along in the sunshine rather than lurk in canal beds nibbling on kelp. Even the ones that've been down there for years can't resist our lures of bright, shining new bells cast out under the shade of a bridge.

I've met a bicycle I like. Now what?

Congratulations! You're starting on the journey of a lifetime. The first stages of bonding are the most important. Some of our bicycles latch on to their new owners immediately, but some require a bit more coaxing to make up their minds. Our trainers will work with you and your new bicycle for an afternoon and let you know if the bicycle's ready to be taken home.

Will I be able to take my bicycle home immediately?

That depends on how acclimated the bicycle is to human interaction. Most of the bicycles we show for potential adoption are ready to go home today, or nearly so. But occasionally we may show a bicycle that still needs a few weeks of socialization before it's ready to leave the Center.

If this bicycle is safe to adopt, why did someone throw it away?

Who can fathom the mind of a drunk stumbling the streets of Amsterdam, pant leg caught in a chain or shin struck by a pedal one time too many? Over 15,000 bicycles are fished out of the canals of Amsterdam each year. Only a small fraction of those were originally dangerous, and most feral bicycles we've recovered have been rehabilitated successfully. But dearie, you couldn't imagine what it does to the psyche. Some of our most feral bicycles stay crouched in the pool for weeks, chasing minnows in their dreams and springing saltwater leaks and snapping at the trainers. We usually catch those cases early. There have been only one or two incidents of bicycles who were too clever for our trainers and sent home with unsuspecting adopters.

Wait. Are you *sure* this bicycle is safe for adoption?

Most certainly.

What happens if there are problems when I get my bicycle home?

Small accidents are expected, particularly as a bicycle gets accustomed to a new home. You may find tire scuffs on the hallway walls, for instance, or skids on the hardwoods. Particularly unhappy bikes may leave chain grease on the curtains, or even gouge the walls with their pedals. Our trainers can schedule house visits in these cases, though that is seldom necessary. Please call the Center's direct number in case of any extreme emergency.

What constitutes an extreme emergency?

We're sure you'll know in the moment.

What do you do with bicycles that are too feral for adoption?

At Maaike's Center For Bicycles Raised By Fishes, we don't believe in putting down the beasties, no matter how feral they may seem. You may have met Willa, our mint green Omafiets with the prettily swept back handlebars, her leather grips nibbled away and wire basket rusted after so long in the canals. She's no longer reliant on the pools, but she's not entirely safe. She does seem to like the office, where the morning light looks like water. When her bell rings, it's so distant and wet that you might think for a moment she's still at the bottom of the canal.

• • •

Sweetheart? Ah, good, you found our brochure. Any questions? Good.

What do you think of this pretty thing? She looks so quick, doesn't she, with her shiny chrome fenders and fresh paint? And I think she likes you; look how she's nuzzling. Why don't you take her for a spin 'round the courtyard? Now aren't you a pair! I feel like I'm at a family reunion.

Of course, she's yours to take home today if you like. She's been rehabilitated for weeks, just waiting for the right one to come along and give her some love. Now, just sign right here—and here—and I'll send you on down to speak with the trainers.

Off you go then, just down the hall. You'll be perfect for each other.

Now sit, Willa. Who's a good girl? I'll just go bring you a plate of kelp, won't I, and then we'll have a bath. Now there's a sweetheart.

BOOK REVIEWS

Cycling to Asylum by Su J. Sokol (Deux Voiliers, 2014)

Reviewed by Alexandrea Flynn

This near-future dystopian novel is the compelling feminist tale of the Wolfes, a bicycling family from Brooklyn who are forced to flee the police state that the USA has become. Cycling is central to Laek & Janie's lives. It's how they commute to work, burn off steam, and embody their activist ideals. In this future New York, where gated neighborhoods and subcutaneous identity chips are the norm, simply being cyclists marks them as radicals. Cycling is also central to the bedtime stories Janie tells their two children, Siri and Simon. The novel also contains evocative descriptions of bicycling in a variety of settings. There is some naked cycling too.

The first few chapters switch between Laek and Janie as narrators, which helps establish how egalitarian their relationship is. The perspective change also highlights what they share and what they hide from each other. I would have been content with two point of view characters, but the author also adds chapters from both Siri and Simon's perspectives. At first I found this rather jarring and annoying, particularly as the language in Simon's chapters is quite childish, but eventually I came to appreciate the emotional depth and tension they provided.

Laek's shady past creates the suspense in part one of the novel. A violent attack at the hands of the police stirs up past torture and sexual traumas and leaves Laek battered and psychologically broken. When Laek is finally able to prove to Janie that their family is in real danger she agrees to the radical step of moving to the "international sanctuary city" of Montréal to apply for refugee status. As a Canadian reader I found the future Canada of the book appealing, but overly optimistic.

The novel is understated in its feminism by portraying the Wolfes as a loving couple whose sex life is playful and healthy without being boring. Laek's bisexuality is not an issue in their marriage. His friendship with Philip, a former lover, is a source of strength for both Laek and Janie. Laek's emotions aren't stifled by the boundaries of traditional masculinity.

The book is in two parts, which take place in Brooklyn and Montréal. Each has a significant climax of action and emotional tension. This was a compelling read, with only a few instances where I was distracted from the story; most of these were due to moments of heavy handed moralizing or incidents where I had trouble suspending my disbelief. The book is timely in its coverage of both police brutality and concerns about a surveillance-obsessed government in the USA.

Sherwood Nation by Benjamin Parzybok (Small Beer Press, 2014)

Reviewed by Sara Tretter

My favorite sub-genre of fiction is *near*-apocalyptic tales, like Octavia Butler's *Parable of the Sower* or David Mitchell's *The Bone Clocks*. Stories that explore a society that's not entirely destroyed, but is beginning to seriously unravel.

In Ben Parzybok's *Sherwood Nation*, drought has cut off the western U.S. from everything east of the Rockies, and cities are left to fend largely for themselves.

Renee, a young barista and fledgling activist in SE Portland, is caught on camera trying to stop a truck filled with stolen water. Rather than flee, she gives the water to thirsty bystanders, earning immediate notoriety and the handle "Maid Marian."

The book is draped on a Robin Hood frame—Maid Marian escapes to Northeast Portland, forms a band of Merry Men comprising various characters from the neighborhood, and emerges as the leader of the self-proclaimed micro-nation of Sherwood. Her Rangers patrol the area on bikes, deliver water, and keep peace on the streets. Meanwhile in downtown Portland, the mayor (this tale's Sherriff of Nottingham) fumbles through city council meetings and plans his revenge on Maid Marian.

What's thrilling about this kind of fiction is that terrifying sense of, "I could totally see this happening." A drought, a city struggling to maintain services, poor neighborhoods being cut loose—this all works. But I grew less engaged as the story unfolded. A young, hipster barista arriving in a poverty-stricken neighborhood and transforming it into a functional nation, with herself at the helm, within a week? The improbability of it kept taking me out of the narrative.

It's fun to imagine a utopia where bikes run the streets and a brilliant woman runs the government. And if you're into tales that explore the beginning of society's breakdown, you'll probably enjoy this book. But as Maid Marian cobbles together a government and builds an infrastructure at an impossibly quick pace, the story, while still a fun read, loses the plausibility needed to live up to its premise.

Brown Girl in the Ring by Nalo Hopkinson (Warner Books, 1998)

Reviewed by Julie Brooks

If you're into socially conscious, urban-fantasy fiction framed by an enthralling blend of Afro-Caribbean mythology and spirituality with a bicycle mentioned along the way, Nalo Hopkinson's book, *Brown Girl in the Ring,* is sure to satisfy. Set in a not-too-far-in-the-future dystopian Toronto, where "the rich and privileged have fled the city, barricaded it behind roadblocks, and left it to crumble," Hopkinson's debut novel, published in 1998, chronicles the tense and sometimes tenuous spiritual, emotional, and intellectual journey of a young woman trying to figure out who she is in the world. Ti-Jeanne, the story's protagonist, is a mother, daughter, granddaughter, and lover existing at the complicated and contentious intersection of these various relationships in her life. An unwed mother ambivalently longing for the affections of her baby's charming, drug-addicted father, living with her medicine woman grandmother, struggling to understand her ability to see "with more than sight," and enduring a pantheon of uninvited spirits forcing themselves upon her, Ti-Jeanne's life is wrought with unambiguous turmoil and confusion. And yet, she powerfully prevails in an unsentimental climax.

The overall plot of *Brown Girl in the Ring* provocatively calls attention to social status, social class, economic inequalities, and racism. And the bicycle appears briefly as the primary mode of transportation in Ti-Jeanne's escape beyond the city limits. Admittedly, I set out reading this book wearing my Little Package cycling cap, hoping that the bicycle would hold more sway than it did. Of course, as the book was published in 1998, it has only been within the last decade that the bicycle has appeared in literature as a vehicle, both literally and metaphorically, of and for social change. Still, if I had the opportunity to sit down with Nalo Hopkinson today and make some suggestions about how she might contemporize her novel for a bicycle-minded audience, I might propose that she weave into the storyline of the escape a thread about class and transportation, power and personal control, strategically situating the bicycle in such a way as to highlight yet another element of the inequities she is already uncovering and illuminating.

Parable of the Sower by Octavia E. Butler (Four Walls Eight Windows, 1993)

Reviewed by Aaron M. Wilson

Octavia E. Butler (1947–2006) was a genius, a gifted storyteller. Her prophetic science fiction, steeped in class struggles, race wars, and gender inequities, reads as warning to future generations.

Parable of the Sower is a story of hope and empathy. There is a lot wrong with the society in which Lauren Olamina, the story's narrator, lives. The story begins with Lauren living with her family in a walled community. The streets are filled with poverty-induced violence. If the characters travel beyond the walls, they take guns and ride bikes. Gasoline is too expensive, so automobiles are rare. On a bike, they can ride quickly by the starved and drug-addled who lay in the streets waiting for easy pray.

In the first half of the book, these bike rides are frequent. Those that live behind protection of the walls use bikes to conduct business with other such communities. They also ride for recreation and training. They ride out to learn how to handle firearms and for target practice. However, if you are looking for a bike-focused read, the bike scenes are underplayed. Bikes are for transportation. The narrator pays very little attention to bikes and bike culture. As a writer, I feel there is room for some fan-fiction to account for the life of a bike mechanic in Butler's world.

The reason to read *Parable of the Sower* is to challenge your worldview of the now. We live in scary times. Systematic racism and the murder of black men and black women are at an unprecedented high. Corporations have taken over our government and busted unions in many states, including Wisconsin, where I live. If we are not careful, if we cannot cultivate empathy for one another, we are doomed to Butler's future.

We would be doomed just like Lauren's walled community. A gang of drug addicts destroys the walled community. However, Lauren was ready. She saw it coming. She had prepared an emergency bag to help her survive. As a survivor afflicted with hyper-empathy, she sets out pragmatically and full of hope to sow and to shape a new society she calls Earthseed: a new society destined to take root in the stars.

I Am the Cheese by Robert Cormier (Pantheon, 1977)

Reviewed by Emily June Street

Given the title *I Am the Cheese*, you'd be forgiven for thinking this a light or funny YA book. But, since it is written by

Robert Cormier, you'd know better. Cormier brought his dark edginess to the YA genre in the 1970s, but this serious book feels relevant even four decades later.

I Am the Cheese tells the story of Adam Farmer, a socially awkward teenager embarking on an impromptu bike trek from Monument, Massachusetts, 150 miles to Rutterberg, Vermont, where he plans to reunite with his father.

The bike trek scenes alternate with a story told in transcripts of sessions between Adam and a therapist/interrogator named only as "T." It soon becomes clear that the events of the bike trek mirror the revelations from Adam's past detailed in the transcripts, and the two realities blur in strange and devious ways.

Cormier creates a poignant—if unreliable—main character. Adam's tale is riveting, and he has quite a past to reveal. His story tackles issues of identity and memory, lies, and truths. Everything he has learned to trust in his short life falls away.

This is a tricky chameleon of a book. At first it appears to be a psychological thriller, but it has so many layers that categorizing it is difficult. In one interpretation, it is bicycle science fiction: a vivid transmutation of one boy's inner life into an external reality held together by his bicycle journey.

The one bright point in an increasingly dark story is Adam's relationship to his bicycle. From the beginning, the bicycle ("old-fashioned, no speeds, no fenders . . . brakes that don't always work and the handlebars with cracked rubber grips,") appears to offer Adam a means to achieve his goals and a sense of freedom. Wheelers will enjoy the striking descriptions of cycling, both the pleasures and the perils.

Adam's relationship to his bicycle serves as a symbol, too, for his relationship to himself. When he's pedaling and he "lets himself join the wind," he feels unencumbered, confident in his ability to cover the terrain and meet his goals.

Slowly, the trek—and Adam's relationship to himself—devolve. By the time his bicycle gets stolen, he can trust nothing, not even his own perceptions. At the same time, in the parallel transcript story, the therapist grows increasingly manipulative and threatening.

In a startling, indeterminate conclusion, the reader is left with Adam still pedaling, pedaling, pedaling on his battered bike. This reader hopes that the healing power of riding will help Adam recover from the traumas he has suffered.

The Rolling Stones by Robert A. Heinlein (Charles Scribner's Sons, 1952)

Reviewed by Dave Dean

I hate the Rolling Stones. I mean the rock band. I justify this hatred on the basis of cultural appropriation, but I actually dislike Mick Jagger's face—he perpetually looks like he's struggling to void his bowels. I've always hated Heinlein, too, due to rampant sexism in his work. In *The Moon is a Harsh Mistress* (1966), Wyoh, a female revolutionary, does little other than take orders and have things explained to her by men. In Heinlein's most famous work, *Stranger in a Strange Land* (1961), a female character suggests that "nine times out of ten when a woman gets raped it's partly her own fault." Sheesh.

Sexism is not such an issue in *The Rolling Stones*. The book is a family space adventure that starts on the moon and proceeds to Mars and beyond. The father/captain, Roger Stone, is not always the focus. His wife, Edith, is a courageous doctor to whom the family defers in medical and ethical matters. Grandmother Hazel is a gifted engineer and a courageous eighty-five year old woman. She routinely outsmarts and criticizes her son. (Hazel appears in *The Moon is a Harsh Mistress*, set on the moon 73 years before, as a twelve year old rebel. As Hazel "aged backward" between 1952 and 1966, Heinlein's attitude toward women seems to have devolved too.) The teenage daughter, Meade Stone, seems to exist mainly to prepare meals and ask whether she's pretty. Stone sons Castor and Pollux are gifted kids who manipulate adult authority figures, including Roger. When it counts, though, the Stone family hangs together.

The book contains lots of detailed space engineering and physics descriptions. Those details Heinlein worked on with his wife Virginia, who was a real-life chemist, biochemist, and engineer. Castor and Pollux start a business importing bicycles (later pets*) to sell on Mars. Bikes are a common sense plan, given the difficulty of transporting fuel and motor vehicles over such a great distance (if we assume providing air, water, and calories to bike riders would be more efficient.) Modified bikes might also be a good way of preserving bone density and muscle mass in low gravity environments, since the Heinleins' idea that low gravity would slow the aging process has been proven false.

I still hate the Rolling Stones, and I usually hate Heinlein too, but I have to admit: *The Rolling Stones* is alright.

*For any *Star Trek* fans: Tribbles are a rip-off of the flatcats from this book. The author of the *Star Trek* episode let Heinlein know, but all RAH asked for was an autographed copy of the script. Pretty cool. Also: I want a flatcat. (A spayed one.)

TELEVISION REVIEWS

Stranger Things, **Season One (Netflix, 2016)**

Reviewed by JH Roberts

Stranger Things seems like a combination of *Freaks and Geeks*, *Twin Peaks*, and *X-Files*, with a healthy dose of Lovecraft. Because it is a new series, I won't tell you much more about the plot, but it includes a group of pre-teens riding bicycles and fighting monsters. Children on bicycles isn't a new trope, but it is a very eighties one, appearing in films such as *E.T.* and *The Goonies* and in the current throwback comic *Paper Girls*. *Stranger Things* is set in the eighties, so the use of bicycles solidifies the eighties aesthetic of the show. Bicycles function as a socio-economic equalizer between the young, male characters in the show. Will Byers comes from a lower-class household and Mike Wheeler comes from an upper middle-class household. We don't know much about Lucas or Dustin, but no matter where they fall on the economic spectrum, all four boys can travel together. *Dungeons and Dragons* functions as a similar equalizer, but that's for another review. Unfortunately, Eleven doesn't get her own bike, but the group is able to travel around without their parents' knowledge through this form of transportation.

"The Waters of Mars" *Doctor Who* **(2008-2010 Specials)**

Reviewed by JH Roberts

The writers of *Doctor Who* have long trusted that viewers who will believe the show's premise—that there is an extraterrestrial with two hearts who travels through time and space in a police call box—would also believe that women, POC, and people with disabilities can be in positions of power, even in contemporary times (such as Kate Lethbridge-Stewart, director of UNIT). "The Waters of Mars" is one such episode. The date is November 21, 2059. The Earth has barely survived an oil apocalypse and terrible ozone pollution, and the human race looks to the stars and other planets for a new home. Captain Adelaide Brooke commands Bowie Base One, the first human colony on Mars. The Doctor mentions that Captain Brooke devoted her whole life to get there. Despite this tendency towards the idea that women must choose either a professional or a family life, other elements of the episode do not suggest as much. The beginning shows Captain Brooke speaking to her adult daughter, who still resides on Earth. They maintain a relationship despite being on different planets, so whatever she gave up does not appear to be a family. Additionally, the Doctor tells her that her granddaughter will also travel through space, inspired by Captain Brooke. Her great-granddaughter will as well, and down through the generations. When the Doctor, who decides the laws of time are his to control in a very masculinist fashion, saves the captain and two officers to change the future, she saves the future and Earth by sacrificing herself. Female autonomy can resist masculine forms of power even against the "Time Lord Victorious."

On Bowie Base One, even after the oil apocalypse, where the officers worry about using too much of their energy reserves, they did not think to bring bicycles. The domes of the base are connected by long corridors, so throughout the episode, characters are seen running around the base. The Doctor mentions that "you could use bikes in this place," and it is true. While it would take fuel to carry bikes to Mars, it would not take extra fuel to power them once they reached the planet. In this post-petroleum future, still not all humans have realized the utility of transportation fueled by a person's own energy.

ABOUT THE CONTRIBUTORS

Aaron M. Wilson is most notably a writer of short stories. His latest book, *Tree Bomber and Other Stories* contains stories of bike mechanics, guerrilla gardening, and Cthulhu mythos.

Alexandrea Flynn is a lifelong cyclist who wishes there was more fiction featuring cycling and cyclists. She lives in British Columbia, Canada.

Cynthia Marts is an East Coast boricua working her way to literary success on the Best Coast. In her spare time she devours pop-culture and genre fiction like a mogwai after midnight. Follow her on twitter @CynoNym.

Dave Dean is an eighth grade English teacher, a Yale National Initiative fellow, and a punk rock band ("Dave Dean's Musical Forklift.") He is married to the author and bookseller Kris Rose. They live in Tulsa, Oklahoma.

Dylan Siegler is a writer and musician from Los Angeles. He is simultaneously working on a novel, his other writing projects, and his punk and metal music He has multiple albums available for digital purchase under his stage name Resident Useless. Check them out!

Elly Blue is more curious about the future than prepared for it. She edits this volume every year (or so) and would love for you to submit a story to the next one.

Emily June Street writes fiction in Northern California. Her books include *The Velocipede Races*, *The Gantean*, and *Sterling*.

Gretchin Lair is an unrequited astronomer, pretend patient, gentle adventurer, recovering calligrapher, unfinished poet, and obsolete geek. She is allergic to coercion, especially when it is marketed as a benefit. gretchin@scarletstarstudios.com

Jessie Kwak is a freelance writer who loves nothing more than slipping nerdy references into her clients' business copies. She's a recent Portland immigrant, and you can follow her bikey-crafty adventures at Bicitoro.com and on Twitter (@JKwak).

Jim Warrenfeltz is a data, exercise, and story junkie. He is living the rural Pennsylvania utopian dream. Follow him at @jimwantscoffee on Twitter if you want to see his thoughts that aren't fit for family on Facebook.

Julie Brooks is a writer, rider, and wholly fascinated roving researcher of all things bikey in Upstate New York. She is the founder and editor of the zine *Pedal by Pedal* and is working on a novel about pedaling with the Bern.

JH Roberts is PhD student at the University of Georgia, studying medieval literature and pop culture.

Kris Rose lives in Tulsa, Ok with her teacher/musician husband Dave Dean, 4 dogs, 4 cats and 5 chickens. She has previously been published in *Red Truck Review* and *This Land* magazine. She enjoys 70's cinema and 60's garage rock. You can reach her at krisrose99@gmail.com

Leigh Ward-Smith writes, edits, reads, parents, wrangles ducks, gardens, runs, bikes, and takes way too many nature photographs in the midwestern United States. When she's not doing those, you'll most likely find her blogging speculative fiction with a feminist angle at Leigh's Wordsmithery (https://leighswordsmithery.wordpress.com/) or bending her mind around hashtag games and world news at her Twitter handle @1WomanWordsmith

Maddy Spencer is a cartoonist in Portland, Oregon. You can read her webcomic, *Simple, Inelegant*, at simpleinelegantcomic.com and find her other art and writing at maddy-spencer.tumblr.com

Robert Bose enjoys spinning fantastical tales and his short stories have appeared in *nEvermore! Tales of Murder*, *Mystery and the Macabre*, and *AB Negative*. He is working on a couple of supernatural mystery novels while annoying his wife, raising three feral children, ultra-running, and drinking with an amazing group of women trying to put a dent in the universe. You can find him online at https://www.facebook.com/robertbose, @RobBose and www.robertbose.com.

Sara Tretter lives, writes, and bikes in Portland, OR with her family.

Sarena Ulibarri is a graduate of the Clarion Fantasy and Science Fiction Writers' Workshop and earned an MFA at the University of Colorado at Boulder. Her fiction has appeared in *Lightspeed*, *Fantastic Stories of the Imagination*, *Lakeside Circus*, and elsewhere. She is an assistant editor for *World Weaver Press* and lives in New Mexico near some gorgeous desert bike paths.

SUBSCRIBE TO EVERYTHING WE PUBLISH!

Do you love what Microcosm publishes?

Do you want us to publish more great stuff?

Would you like to receive each new title as it's published?

Subscribe as a BFF to our new titles and we'll mail them all to you as they are released!

$10-30/mo, pay what you can afford. Include your t-shirt size and your birthday for a possible surprise!

microcosmpublishing.com/bff

...AND HELP US GROW YOUR SMALL WORLD!